A Room of One's Own

A Room
of One's Own

VIRGINIA
WOOLF

Annotated and with an introduction
by Susan Gubar

Mark Hussey, General Editor

A Harvest Book • Harcourt, Inc.
Orlando Austin New York San Diego London

www.HarcourtBooks.com

Library of Congress Cataloging-in-Publication Data
Woolf, Virginia, 1882–1941.
A room of one's own/Virginia Woolf;
annotated and with an introduction by Susan Gubar;
Mark Hussey, general editor.—1st Harvest ed.
p.   cm.—(A Harvest Book)
1. Woolf, Virginia, 1882–1941—Authorship.   2. Literature—Women authors—
History and criticism—Theory, etc.   3. Women and literature—Great Britain.
4. Women authors—Economic conditions.   5. Women authors—Social conditions.
6. Authorship—Sex differences.   I. Gubar, Susan, 1944–   II. Title.
PR6045.O72Z474   2005
823'.912—dc22   2005004202
ISBN 978-0156-03041-0

Text set in Garamond MT
Designed by Cathy Riggs

Printed in the United States of America

First edition
DOM 20 19 18 17 16 15 14 13 12

Contents

A Room of One's Own

VIRGINIA WOOLF

VIRGINIA WOOLF was born into what she once described as "a very communicative, literate, letter writing, visiting, articulate, late nineteenth century world." Her parents, Leslie and Julia Stephen, both previously widowed, began their marriage in 1878 with four young children: Laura (1870–1945), the daughter of Leslie Stephen and his first wife, Harriet Thackeray (1840–1875); and George (1868–1934), Gerald (1870–1937), and Stella Duckworth (1869–1897), the children of Julia Prinsep (1846–1895) and Herbert Duckworth (1833–1870). In the first five years of their marriage, the Stephens had four more children. Their third child, Virginia, was born in 1882, the year her father began work on the monumental *Dictionary of National Biography* that would earn him a knighthood in 1902. Virginia, her sister, Vanessa (1879–1961), and brothers, Thoby (1880–1906) and Adrian (1883–1948), all were born in the tall house at 22 Hyde Park Gate in London where the eight children lived with numerous servants, their eminent and irascible father, and their beautiful mother, who, in Woolf's words, was "in the very centre of that great Cathedral space that was childhood."

Woolf's parents knew many of the intellectual luminaries of the late Victorian era well, counting among their close friends novelists such as George Meredith, Thomas Hardy, and Henry James. Woolf's great-aunt Julia Margaret Cameron was a pioneering photographer who made portraits of the poets Alfred

Tennyson and Robert Browning, of the naturalist Charles Darwin, and of the philosopher and historian Thomas Carlyle, among many others. Beginning in the year Woolf was born, the entire Stephen family moved to Talland House in St. Ives, Cornwall, for the summer. There the younger children would spend their days playing cricket in the garden, frolicking on the beach, or taking walks along the coast, from where they could look out across the bay to the Godrevy lighthouse.

The early years of Woolf's life were marred by traumatic events. When she was thirteen, her mother, exhausted by a punishing schedule of charitable visits among the sick and poor, died from a bout of influenza. Woolf's half sister Stella took over the household responsibilities and bore the brunt of their self-pitying father's sorrow until she escaped into marriage in 1897 with Jack Hills, a young man who had been a favorite of Julia's. Within three months, Stella (who was pregnant) was dead, most likely from peritonitis. In this year, which she called "the first really *lived* year of my life," Woolf began a diary. Over the next twelve years, she would record in its pages her voracious reading, her impressions of people and places, feelings about her siblings, and events in the daily life of the large household.[1]

In addition to the premature deaths of her mother and half sister, there were other miseries in Woolf's childhood. In autobiographical writings and letters, Woolf referred to the sexual abuse she suffered at the hands of her two older half brothers, George and Gerald Duckworth. George, in one instance, explained his behavior to a family doctor as his effort to comfort his half sister for the fatal illness of their father. Sir Leslie died

[1]Woolf's early diary is published as *A Passionate Apprentice: The Early Journals, 1897–1909*, edited by Mitchell A. Leaska. A 1909 notebook discovered in 2002 has been published as *Carlyle's House and Other Sketches*, edited by David Bradshaw (London: Hesperus, 2003).

from cancer in 1904, and shortly thereafter the four Stephen children—Vanessa, Virginia, Thoby, and Adrian—moved together to the then-unfashionable London neighborhood of Bloomsbury. When Thoby Stephen began to bring his Cambridge University friends to the house on Thursday evenings, what would later become famous as the "Bloomsbury Group" began to form.

In an article marking the centenary of her father's birth, Woolf recalled his "allowing a girl of fifteen the free run of a large and quite unexpurgated library"—an unusual opportunity for a Victorian young woman, and evidence of the high regard Sir Leslie had for his daughter's intellectual talents. In her diary, she recorded the many different kinds of books her father recommended to her—biographies and memoirs, philosophy, history, and poetry. Although he believed that women should be "as well educated as men," Woolf's mother held that "to serve is the fulfilment of women's highest nature." The young Stephen children were first taught at home by their mother and father, with little success. Woolf herself received no formal education beyond some classes in Greek and Latin in the Ladies' Department of King's College in London, beginning in the fall of 1897. In 1899 she began lessons in Greek with Clara Pater, sister of the renowned Victorian critic Walter Pater, and in 1902 she was tutored in the classics by Janet Case (who also later involved her in work for women's suffrage). Such homeschooling was a source of some bitterness later in her life, as she recognized the advantages that derived from the expensive educations her brothers and half brothers received at private schools and university. Yet she also realized that her father's encouragement of her obviously keen intellect had given her an eclectic foundation. In the early years of Bloomsbury, she reveled in the opportunity to discuss ideas with her brother Thoby and his friends, among whom were Lytton Strachey, Clive Bell, and

E. M. Forster. From them, she heard, too, about an intense young man named Leonard Woolf, whom she had met briefly when visiting Thoby at Cambridge, and also in 1904 when he came to dinner at Gordon Square just before leaving for Ceylon (now called Sri Lanka), where he was to administer a far-flung outpost of the British Empire.

Virginia Woolf's first publications were unsigned reviews and essays in an Anglo-Catholic newspaper called the *Guardian,* beginning in December 1904. In the fall of 1906, she and Vanessa went with a family friend, Violet Dickinson, to meet their brothers in Greece. The trip was spoiled by Vanessa's falling ill, and when she returned to London, Virginia found both her brother Thoby—who had returned earlier—and her sister seriously ill. After a misdiagnosis by his doctors, Thoby died from typhoid fever on November 20, leaving Virginia to maintain a cheerful front while her sister and Violet Dickinson recovered from their own illnesses. Two days after Thoby's death, Vanessa agreed to marry his close friend Clive Bell.

While living in Bloomsbury, Woolf had begun to write a novel that would go through many drafts before it was published in 1915 as *The Voyage Out.* In these early years of independence, her social circle widened. She became close to the art critic Roger Fry, organizer of the First Post-Impressionist Exhibition in London in 1910, and also entered the orbit of the famed literary hostess Lady Ottoline Morrell (cruelly caricatured as Hermione Roddice in D. H. Lawrence's 1920 novel *Women in Love*). Her political consciousness also began to emerge. In 1910 she volunteered for the movement for women's suffrage. She also participated that February in a daring hoax that embarrassed the British Navy and led to questions being asked in the House of Commons: She and her brother Adrian, together with some other Cambridge friends, gained access to a secret warship by dressing up and posing as the Emperor of Abyssinia and his retinue. The "Dreadnought Hoax" was front-page news, complete with photographs of the phony Ethiopians with flowing robes, blackened faces, and false beards.

To the British establishment, one of the most embarrassing aspects of the Dreadnought affair was that a woman had taken part in the hoax. Vanessa Bell was concerned at what might have happened to her sister had she been discovered on the ship. She was also increasingly worried about Virginia's erratic health, and by the early summer 1910 had discussed with Dr. George Savage, one of the family's doctors, the debilitating headaches her sister suffered; Dr. Savage prescribed several weeks in a nursing home. Another element in Vanessa's concern was that Virginia was twenty-eight and still unmarried. Clive Bell and Virginia had, in fact, engaged in a hurtful flirtation soon after the birth of Vanessa's first child in 1908. Although she had been proposed to twice in 1909 and once in 1911, Virginia had not taken these offers very seriously.

Dropping by Vanessa's house on a July evening in 1911, Virginia met Leonard Woolf, recently back on leave from Ceylon. Soon after this, Leonard became a lodger at the house Virginia shared with Adrian, the economist John Maynard Keynes, and the painter Duncan Grant. Leonard decided to resign from the Colonial Service, hoping that Virginia would agree to marry him. After some considerable hesitation, she did, and they married in August 1912.

By the end of that year, Woolf was again suffering from the tremendous headaches that afflicted her throughout her life, and in 1913 she was again sent to a nursing home for what was then called a "rest cure." In September of that year, she took an overdose of a sleeping drug and was under care until the following spring. In early 1915 she suffered a severe breakdown and was ill throughout most of the year in which her first novel was published.

Despite this difficult beginning, Virginia and Leonard Woolf's marriage eventually settled into a pattern of immense productivity and mutual support. Leonard worked for a time for the Women's Cooperative Guild, and became increasingly involved with advising the Labour Party and writing on international politics, as well as editing several periodicals. Virginia began to establish herself as an important novelist and influential critic. In 1917 the Woolfs set up their own publishing house, the Hogarth Press, in their home in Richmond. Their first publication was *Two Stories*—Leonard's "Three Jews" and Virginia's experimental "The Mark on the Wall." They had decided to make their livings by writing, and in 1919, a few months before Woolf's second novel, *Night and Day,* was published, they bought a cottage in the village of Rodmell in Sussex. After moving back into London from Richmond in 1923, Woolf would spend summers at Monk's House, returning to the social whirl of the city in the fall.

"The Mark on the Wall" was one of a number of what Woolf called "sketches" that she began to write around the time she and Leonard bought their printing press. *Night and Day* was the last of her books to be published in England by another press. In 1919 Hogarth published her short story *Kew Gardens,* with two woodcuts by Vanessa Bell, and two years later came *Monday or Tuesday,* the only collection of her short fiction published in Woolf's lifetime. Her next novel was *Jacob's Room* (1922), a slim elegy to the generation of 1914, and to her beloved brother Thoby, whose life of great promise had also been cut short so suddenly. Woolf had written to her friend Margaret Llewelyn Davies in 1916 that the Great War, as it was then called, was a "preposterous masculine fiction" that made her "steadily more feminist," and in her fiction and nonfiction she began to articulate and illuminate the connections between the patriarchal status quo, the relatively subordinate position of

women, and war making. Thinking about a novel she was calling "The Hours," Woolf wrote in her diary in 1923 that she
wanted to criticize "the social system." Her inclusion in the
novel of a shell-shocked war veteran named Septimus Warren
Smith would confuse many of the early reviewers of her fourth
novel, *Mrs. Dalloway* (1925), but others recognized that Woolf
was breaking new ground in the way she rendered consciousness and her understanding of human subjectivity.

By the time she wrote *Mrs. Dalloway,* Woolf was also a sought-
after essayist and reviewer who, like many of her celebrated
contemporaries, was staking out her own particular piece of
modernist territory. The Hogarth Press published radical young
writers like Katherine Mansfield, T. S. Eliot, and Gertrude Stein.
Approached by Harriet Shaw Weaver with part of the manuscript of James Joyce's *Ulysses* in 1918, the Woolfs turned it down.
Their own small press could not cope with the long and complex manuscript, nor could Leonard Woolf find a commercial
printer willing to risk prosecution for obscenity by producing it.
In 1924 the Hogarth Press became the official English publisher
of the works of Sigmund Freud, translated by Lytton Strachey's
brother James. Woolf's own literary criticism was collected in a
volume published in 1925, *The Common Reader*—a title signaling
her distrust of academics and love of broad, eclectic reading.

The staggering range of Woolf's reading is reflected in the
more than five hundred essays and reviews she published during her lifetime. Her critical writing is concerned not only with
the canonical works of English literature from Chaucer to her
contemporaries, but also ranges widely through lives of the obscure, memoirs, diaries, letters, and biographies. Models of the
form, her essays comprise a body of work that has only recently
begun to attract the kind of recognition her fiction has received.

In 1922 Woolf met "the lovely and gifted aristocrat" Vita
Sackville-West, already a well-known poet and novelist. Their

close friendship slowly turned into a love affair, glowing most intensely from about 1925 to 1928, before modulating into friendship once more in the 1930s. The period of their intimacy was extremely creative for both writers, Woolf publishing essays such as "Mr. Bennett and Mrs. Brown" and "Letter to a Young Poet," as well as three very different novels: *To the Lighthouse* (1927), which evoked her own childhood and had at its center the figure of a modernist woman artist, Lily Briscoe; *Orlando* (1928), a fantastic biography inspired by Vita's own remarkable family history; and *The Waves* (1931), a mystical and profoundly meditative work that pushed Woolf's concept of novel form to its limit. Woolf also published a second *Common Reader* in 1932, and the "biography" of *Flush,* Elizabeth Barrett Browning's dog (1933). She went with Sackville-West to Cambridge in the fall of 1928 to deliver the second of the two lectures on which her great feminist essay *A Room of One's Own* (1929) is based.

As the political situation in Europe in the 1930s moved inexorably to its crisis in 1939, Woolf began to collect newspaper clippings about the relations between the sexes in England, France, Germany, and Italy. The scrapbooks she made became the matrix from which developed the perspectives of her penultimate novel, *The Years* (1937), and the arguments of her pacifist-feminist polemic *Three Guineas* (1938). In 1937 Vanessa's eldest son, Julian Bell, was killed serving as an ambulance driver in the Spanish Civil War. Woolf later wrote to Vanessa that she had written *Three Guineas* partly as an argument with Julian. Her work on *The Years* was grindingly slow and difficult. Ironically, given Woolf's reputation as a highbrow, it became a bestseller in the United States, even being published in an Armed Services edition. While she labored over the novel in 1934, the news came of the death of Roger Fry, one of her oldest and closest friends and the former lover of her sister, Vanessa. Reluctantly, given her distaste for the conventions of biography, Woolf agreed to write his life, which was published in 1940.

In 1939, to relieve the strain of writing Fry's biography, Woolf began to write a memoir, "A Sketch of the Past," which remained unpublished until 1976, when the manuscripts were edited by Jeanne Schulkind for a collection of Woolf's autobiographical writings, *Moments of Being*. Withdrawing with Leonard to Monk's House in Sussex, where they could see the German airplanes flying low overhead on their way to bomb London, Woolf continued to write for peace and correspond with antiwar activists in Europe and the United States. She began to write her last novel, *Between the Acts*, in the spring of 1938, but by early 1941 was dissatisfied with it. Before completing her final revisions, Woolf ended her own life, walking into the River Ouse on the morning of March 28, 1941. To her sister, Vanessa, she wrote, "I can hardly think clearly any more. If I could I would tell you what you and the children have meant to me. I think you know." In her last note to Leonard, she told him he had given her "complete happiness," and asked him to destroy all her papers.

BY THE END of the twentieth century, Virginia Woolf had become an iconic figure, a touchstone for the feminism that revived in the 1960s as well as for the conservative backlash of the 1980s. Hailed by many as a radical writer of genius, she has also been dismissed as a narrowly focused snob. Her image adorns T-shirts, postcards, and even a beer advertisement, while phrases from her writings occur in all kinds of contexts, from peace-march slogans to highbrow book reviews. That Woolf is one of those figures upon whom the myriad competing narratives of twentieth- and twenty-first-century Western culture inscribe themselves is testified to by the enormous number of biographical works about her published in the decades since her nephew Quentin Bell broke the ground in 1972 with his two-volume biography of his aunt.

Argument continues about the work and life of Virginia Woolf: about her experience of incest, her madness, her class attitudes, her sexuality, the difficulty of her prose, her politics, her feminism, and her legacy. Perhaps, though, these words from her essay "How Should One Read a Book?" are our best guide: "The only advice, indeed, that one person can give another about reading is to take no advice, to follow your own instincts, to use your own reason, to come to your own conclusions."

—MARK HUSSEY, GENERAL EDITOR

Information is arranged in this order: 1. Virginia Woolf's family and her works; 2. Cultural and political events; 3. Significant publications and works of art.

1878   Marriage of Woolf's parents, Leslie Stephen (1832–1904) and Julia Prinsep Duckworth (née Jackson) (1846–1895). Leslie Stephen publishes *Samuel Johnson*, first volume in the English Men of Letters series. England at war in Afghanistan.

1879   Vanessa Stephen (Bell) born (d. 1961). Edward Burne-Jones paints Julia Stephen as the Virgin Mary in *The Annunciation*. Leslie Stephen, *Hours in a Library*, 3rd series.
Somerville and Lady Margaret Hall Colleges for women founded at Oxford University.
Anglo-Zulu war in South Africa.

1880   Thoby Stephen born (d. 1906).
William Gladstone becomes prime minister for second time. First Boer War begins (1880–81). Deaths of Gustave Flaubert (b. 1821) and George Eliot (b. 1819). Lytton Strachey born (d. 1932).
Fyodor Dostoyevsky, *The Brothers Karamazov*.

1881   Leslie Stephen buys lease of Talland House, St. Ives, Cornwall.
Cambridge University Tripos exams opened to women.
Henrik Ibsen, *Ghosts;* Henry James, *The Portrait of a Lady, Washington Square;* Christina Rossetti, *A Pageant and Other Poems;* D. G. Rossetti, *Ballads and Sonnets;* Oscar Wilde, *Poems.*

1882   Adeline Virginia Stephen (Virginia Woolf) born January 25. Leslie Stephen begins work as editor of the *Dictionary of National Biography* (*DNB*); publishes *The Science of Ethics.* The Stephen family spends its first summer at Talland House.
Married Women's Property Act enables women to buy, sell, and own property and keep their own earnings. Triple Alliance between Germany, Italy, and Austria. Phoenix Park murders of British officials in Dublin, Ireland. James Joyce born (d. 1941). Death of Charles Darwin (b. 1809).

1883   Adrian Leslie Stephen born (d. 1948). Julia Stephen's *Notes from Sick Rooms* published.
Olive Schreiner, *The Story of an African Farm;* Robert Louis Stevenson, *Treasure Island.*

1884   Leslie Stephen delivers the Clark Lectures at Cambridge University.
Third Reform Act extends the franchise in England. Friedrich Engels, *The Origin of the Family, Private Property and the State;* John Ruskin, *The Storm-Cloud of the Nineteenth Century;* Mark Twain, *The Adventures of Huckleberry Finn.*

1885   First volume of Leslie Stephen's *Dictionary of National Biography* published.

Redistribution Act further extends the franchise in England. Ezra Pound born (d. 1972); D. H. Lawrence born (d. 1930).

George Meredith, *Diana of the Crossways;* Émile Zola, *Germinal.*

1887   Queen Victoria's Golden Jubilee.

Arthur Conan Doyle, *A Study in Scarlet;* H. Rider Haggard, *She;* Thomas Hardy, *The Woodlanders.*

1891   Leslie Stephen gives up the *DNB* editorship. Laura Stephen (1870–1945) is placed in an asylum.

William Gladstone elected prime minister of England a fourth time.

Thomas Hardy, *Tess of the D'Urbervilles;* Oscar Wilde, *The Picture of Dorian Gray.*

1895   Death of Julia Stephen.

Armenian Massacres in Turkey. Discovery of X-rays by William Röntgen; Guglielmo Marconi discovers radio; invention of the cinematograph. Trials of Oscar Wilde.

Thomas Hardy, *Jude the Obscure;* H. G. Wells, *The Time Machine;* Oscar Wilde, *The Importance of Being Earnest.*

1896   Vanessa Stephen begins drawing classes three afternoons a week.

Death of William Morris (b. 1834); F. Scott Fitzgerald born (d. 1940).

Anton Chekhov, *The Seagull.*

1897   Woolf attends Greek and history classes at King's
College, London, and begins to keep a regular diary.
Vanessa, Virginia, and Thoby watch Queen Victoria's
Diamond Jubilee procession. Stella Duckworth (b. 1869)
marries Jack Hills in April, but dies in July. Gerald Duck-
worth (1870–1937) establishes a publishing house.
Paul Gauguin, *Where Do We Come From? What Are We?
Where Are We Going?*; Bram Stoker, *Dracula*.

1898   Spanish-American War (1898–99). Marie Curie discovers radium. Death of Stéphane Mallarmé (b. 1842).
H. G. Wells, *The War of the Worlds*; Oscar Wilde, *The Ballad of Reading Gaol*.

1899   Woolf begins Latin and Greek lessons with Clara Pater.
Thoby Stephen goes up to Trinity College, Cambridge
University, entering with Lytton Strachey, Leonard
Woolf (1880–1969), and Clive Bell (1881–1964).
The Second Boer War begins (1899–1902) in South
Africa. Ernest Hemingway born (d. 1961).

1900   Woolf and Vanessa attend the Trinity College Ball at
Cambridge University.
Deaths of Friedrich Nietzsche (b. 1844), John Ruskin
(b. 1819), and Oscar Wilde (b. 1854).
Sigmund Freud, *The Interpretation of Dreams*.

1901   Vanessa enters Royal Academy Schools.
Queen Victoria dies January 22. Edward VII becomes
king. Marconi sends messages by wireless telegraphy
from Cornwall to Newfoundland.

1902 Woolf begins classics lessons with Janet Case. Adrian Stephen enters Trinity College, Cambridge University. Leslie Stephen is knighted.

Joseph Conrad, *Heart of Darkness*; Henry James, *The Wings of the Dove*; William James, *The Varieties of Religious Experience*.

1903 The Wright Brothers fly a biplane 852 feet. Women's Social and Political Union founded in England by Emmeline Pankhurst.

1904 Sir Leslie Stephen dies. George Duckworth (1868–1934) marries Lady Margaret Herbert. The Stephen children—Vanessa, Virginia, Thoby, and Adrian—move to 46 Gordon Square, in the Bloomsbury district of London. Woolf contributes to F. W. Maitland's biography of her father. Leonard Woolf comes to dine before sailing for Ceylon. Woolf travels in Italy and France. Her first publication is an unsigned review in the *Guardian*, a church weekly.

"Empire Day" inaugurated in London and in Britain's colonies.

Anton Chekhov, *The Cherry Orchard*; Henry James, *The Golden Bowl*.

1905 Woolf begins teaching weekly adult education classes at Morley College. Thoby invites Cambridge friends to their home for "Thursday Evenings"—the beginnings of the Bloomsbury Group. Woolf travels with Adrian to Portugal and Spain. The Stephens visit Cornwall for the first time since their mother's death.

Revolution in Russia.

Albert Einstein, *Special Theory of Relativity;* E. M. Forster, *Where Angels Fear to Tread;* Sigmund Freud, *Essays in the Theory of Sexuality;* Edith Wharton, *The House of Mirth;* Oscar Wilde, *De Profundis.*

1906   The Stephens travel to Greece. Vanessa and Thoby fall ill. Thoby dies November 20; on November 22, Vanessa agrees to marry Clive Bell.
Deaths of Paul Cézanne (b. 1839) and Henrik Ibsen (b. 1828). Samuel Beckett born (d. 1989).

1907   Woolf moves with her brother Adrian to Fitzroy Square. Vanessa marries Clive Bell.
First Cubist exhibition in Paris. W. H. Auden born (d. 1973).
Joseph Conrad, *The Secret Agent;* E. M. Forster, *The Longest Journey;* Edmund Gosse, *Father and Son;* Pablo Picasso, *Demoiselles d'Avignon.*

1908   Birth of Vanessa Bell's first child, Julian. Woolf travels to Italy with Vanessa and Clive Bell.
Herbert Asquith becomes prime minister.
E. M. Forster, *A Room with a View;* Gertrude Stein, *Three Lives.*

1909   Woolf receives a legacy of £2,500 on the death of her Quaker aunt, Caroline Emelia Stephen. Lytton Strachey proposes marriage to Woolf, but they both quickly realize this would be a mistake. Woolf meets Lady Ottoline Morrell for the first time. She travels to the Wagner festival in Bayreuth.
Chancellor of the Exchequer David Lloyd George (1863–1945) introduces a "People's Budget," taxing

wealth to pay for social reforms. A constitutional crisis ensues when the House of Lords rejects it. Death of George Meredith (b. 1828).

Filippo Marinetti, "The Founding and Manifesto of Futurism"; Henri Matisse, *Dance.*

1910   Woolf participates in the Dreadnought Hoax. She volunteers for the cause of women's suffrage. Birth of Vanessa Bell's second child, Quentin (d. 1996).

First Post-Impressionist Exhibition ("Manet and the Post-Impressionists") organized by Roger Fry (1866–1934) at the Grafton Galleries in London. Edward VII dies May 6. George V becomes king. Death of Leo Tolstoy (b. 1828).

E. M. Forster, *Howards End;* Igor Stravinsky, *The Firebird.*

1911   Woolf rents Little Talland House in Sussex. Leonard Woolf returns from Ceylon; in November, he, Adrian Stephen, John Maynard Keynes (1883–1946), Woolf, and Duncan Grant (1885–1978) share a house together at Brunswick Square in London.

Ernest Rutherford makes first model of atomic structure. Rupert Brooke, *Poems;* Joseph Conrad, *Under Western Eyes;* D. H. Lawrence, *The White Peacock;* Katherine Mansfield, *In a German Pension;* Ezra Pound, *Canzoni;* Edith Wharton, *Ethan Frome.*

1912   Woolf leases Asheham House in Sussex. Marries Leonard on August 10; they move to Clifford's Inn, London.

Captain Robert Scott's expedition reaches the South Pole, but he and his companions die on the return

A Room of One's Own

journey. The *Titanic* sinks. Second Post-Impression-
ist Exhibition, for which Leonard Woolf serves as
secretary.
Marcel Duchamp, *Nude Descending a Staircase;* Wassily
Kandinsky, *Concerning the Spiritual in Art;* Thomas
Mann, *Death in Venice;* George Bernard Shaw, *Pygmalion.*

1913   *The Voyage Out* manuscript delivered to Gerald Duckworth. Woolf enters a nursing home in July; in September, she attempts suicide.
Roger Fry founds the Omega Workshops.
Sigmund Freud, *Totem and Taboo;* D. H. Lawrence, *Sons
and Lovers;* Marcel Proust, *Du côté de chez Swann;* Igor
Stravinsky, *Le Sacre du printemps.*

1914   Leonard Woolf, *The Wise Virgins;* he reviews Freud's
The Psychopathology of Everyday Life.
World War I ("The Great War") begins in August.
Home Rule Bill for Ireland passed.
Clive Bell, *Art;* James Joyce, *Dubliners;* Wyndham Lewis
et al., "Vorticist Manifesto" (in *Blast*); Gertrude Stein,
Tender Buttons.

1915   *The Voyage Out,* Woolf's first novel, published by Duck-
worth. In April the Woolfs move to Hogarth House in
Richmond. Woolf begins again to keep a regular diary.
First Zeppelin attack on London. Death of Rupert
Brooke (b. 1887).
Joseph Conrad, *Victory;* Ford Madox Ford, *The Good Sol-
dier;* D. H. Lawrence, *The Rainbow;* Dorothy Richardson,
Pointed Roofs.

1916   Woolf discovers Charleston, where her sister, Vanessa (no longer living with her husband, Clive), moves in October with her sons, Julian and Quentin, and Duncan Grant (with whom she is in love) and David Garnett (with whom Duncan is in love).

Easter Rising in Dublin. Death of Henry James (b. 1843).

Albert Einstein, *General Theory of Relativity;* James Joyce, *A Portrait of the Artist as a Young Man;* Dorothy Richardson, *Backwater.*

1917   The Hogarth Press established by Leonard and Virginia Woolf in Richmond. Their first publication is their own *Two Stories,* with woodcuts by Dora Carrington (1893–1932).

Russian Bolshevik Revolution destroys the rule of the czar. The United States enters the European war.

T. S. Eliot, *Prufrock and Other Observations;* Sigmund Freud, *Introduction to Psychoanalysis;* Carl Jung, *The Unconscious;* Dorothy Richardson, *Honeycomb;* W. B. Yeats, *The Wild Swans at Coole.*

1918   Woolf meets T. S. Eliot (1888–1965). Harriet Shaw Weaver comes to tea with the manuscript of James Joyce's *Ulysses.* Vanessa Bell and Duncan Grant's daughter, Angelica Garnett, born; her paternity is kept secret from all but a very few intimates.

Armistice signed November 11; Parliamentary Reform Act gives votes in Britain to women of thirty and older and to all men.

G. M. Hopkins, *Poems;* James Joyce, *Exiles;* Katherine Mansfield, *Prelude* (Hogarth Press); Marcel Proust, *À l'ombre des jeunes filles en fleurs;* Lytton Strachey, *Eminent Victorians;* Rebecca West, *The Return of the Soldier.*

1919 The Woolfs buy Monk's House in Sussex. Woolf's second novel, *Night and Day,* is published by Duckworth. Her essay "Modern Novels" (republished in 1925 as "Modern Fiction") appears in the *Times Literary Supplement; Kew Gardens* published by Hogarth Press.
Bauhaus founded by Walter Gropius in Weimar. Sex Disqualification (Removal) Act opens many professions and public offices to women. Election of first woman member of parliament, Nancy Astor. Treaty of Versailles imposes harsh conditions on postwar Germany, opposed by John Maynard Keynes, who writes *The Economic Consequences of the Peace.* League of Nations created. T. S. Eliot, "Tradition and the Individual Talent," *Poems;* Dorothy Richardson, *The Tunnel, Interim;* Robert Wiene, *The Cabinet of Dr. Caligari* (film).

1920 The Memoir Club, comprising thirteen original members of the Bloomsbury Group, meets for the first time. *The Voyage Out* and *Night and Day* are published in the United States by George H. Doran.
Mohandas Gandhi initiates mass passive resistance against British rule in India.
T. S. Eliot, *The Sacred Wood;* Sigmund Freud, *Beyond the Pleasure Principle;* Roger Fry, *Vision and Design;* D. H. Lawrence, *Women in Love;* Katherine Mansfield, *Bliss and Other Stories;* Ezra Pound, *Hugh Selwyn Mauberley;* Marcel Proust, *Le Côté de Guermantes I;* Edith Wharton, *The Age of Innocence.*

1921 Woolf's short story collection *Monday or Tuesday* published by Hogarth Press, which will from this time publish all her books in England. The book is also published in the United States by Harcourt Brace, which from now on is her American publisher.

Aldous Huxley, *Crome Yellow;* Pablo Picasso, *Three Musicians;* Luigi Pirandello, *Six Characters in Search of an Author;* Marcel Proust, *Le Côté de Guermantes II, Sodome et Gomorrhe I;* Dorothy Richardson, *Deadlock;* Lytton Strachey, *Queen Victoria.*

1922   *Jacob's Room* published. Woolf meets Vita Sackville-West (1892–1962) for the first time.

Bonar Law elected prime minister. Mussolini comes to power in Italy. Irish Free State established. British Broadcasting Company (BBC) formed. Discovery of Tutankhamen's tomb in Egypt. Death of Marcel Proust (b. 1871).

T. S. Eliot, *The Waste Land;* James Joyce, *Ulysses;* Katherine Mansfield, *The Garden Party;* Marcel Proust, *Sodome et Gomorrhe II;* Ludwig Wittgenstein, *Tractatus Logico-Philosophicus.*

1923   The Woolfs travel to Spain, stopping in Paris on the way home. Hogarth Press publishes *The Waste Land.*

Stanley Baldwin succeeds Bonar Law as prime minister. Death of Katherine Mansfield (b. 1888).

Mina Loy, *Lunar Baedeker;* Marcel Proust, *La Prisonnière;* Dorothy Richardson, *Revolving Lights;* Rainer Maria Rilke, *Duino Elegies.*

1924   The Woolfs move to Tavistock Square. Woolf lectures on "Character in Fiction" to the Heretics Society at Cambridge University.

The Labour Party takes office for the first time under

the leadership of Ramsay MacDonald but is voted out within the year. Death of Joseph Conrad (b. 1857).

E. M. Forster, *A Passage to India;* Thomas Mann, *The Magic Mountain.*

1925 *Mrs. Dalloway* and *The Common Reader* published. Woolf stays with Vita Sackville-West at her house, Long Barn, for the first time.

Nancy Cunard, *Parallax;* F. Scott Fitzgerald, *The Great Gatsby;* Ernest Hemingway, *In Our Time;* Adolf Hitler, *Mein Kampf;* Franz Kafka, *The Trial;* Alain Locke, ed., *The New Negro;* Marcel Proust, *Albertine disparue;* Dorothy Richardson, *The Trap;* Gertrude Stein, *The Making of Americans.*

1926 Woolf lectures on "How Should One Read a Book?" at Hayes Court School. "Cinema" published in *Arts* (New York), "Impassioned Prose" in *Times Literary Supplement,* and "On Being Ill" in *New Criterion.* Meets Gertrude Stein (1874–1946).

The General Strike in support of mine workers in England lasts nearly two weeks.

Ernest Hemingway, *The Sun Also Rises;* Langston Hughes, *The Weary Blues;* Franz Kafka, *The Castle;* A. A. Milne, *Winnie-the-Pooh.*

1927 *To the Lighthouse,* "The Art of Fiction," "Poetry, Fiction and the Future," and "Street Haunting" published. The Woolfs travel with Vita Sackville-West and her husband, Harold Nicolson, to Yorkshire to see the total eclipse of the sun. They buy their first car.

Charles Lindbergh flies the Atlantic solo.

E. M. Forster, *Aspects of the Novel;* Ernest Hemingway, *Men without Women;* Franz Kafka, *Amerika;* Marcel

Proust, *Le Temps retrouvé;* Gertrude Stein, *Four Saints in Three Acts.*

1928   *Orlando: A Biography* published. In October, Woolf delivers two lectures at Cambridge on which she will base *A Room of One's Own.* Femina-Vie Heureuse prize awarded to *To the Lighthouse.*

The Equal Franchise Act gives the vote to all women over twenty-one. Sound films introduced. Death of Thomas Hardy (b. 1840).

Djuna Barnes, *Ladies Almanack;* Radclyffe Hall, *The Well of Loneliness;* D. H. Lawrence, *Lady Chatterley's Lover;* Evelyn Waugh, *Decline and Fall;* W. B. Yeats, *The Tower.*

1929   *A Room of One's Own* published. "Women and Fiction" in *The Forum* (New York).

Labour Party returned to power under Prime Minister MacDonald. Discovery of penicillin. Museum of Modern Art opens in New York. Wall Street crash.

William Faulkner, *The Sound and the Fury;* Ernest Hemingway, *A Farewell to Arms;* Nella Larsen, *Passing.*

1930   Woolf meets the pioneering composer, writer, and suffragette Ethel Smyth (1858–1944), with whom she forms a close friendship.

Death of D. H. Lawrence (b. 1885).

W. H. Auden, *Poems;* T. S. Eliot, *Ash Wednesday;* William Faulkner, *As I Lay Dying;* Sigmund Freud, *Civilisation and Its Discontents.*

1931   *The Waves* is published. First of six articles by Woolf about London published in *Good Housekeeping;* "Introductory Letter" to *Life As We Have Known It.* Lectures to London branch of National Society for Women's Service on "Professions for Women." Meets John Lehmann (1907–1987), who will become a partner in the Hogarth Press.

Growing financial crisis throughout Europe and beginning of the Great Depression.

1932   *The Common Reader, Second Series* and "Letter to a Young Poet" published. Woolf invited to give the 1933 Clark Lectures at Cambridge, which she declines.

Death of Lytton Strachey (b. 1880).

Aldous Huxley, *Brave New World*.

1933   *Flush: A Biography,* published. The Woolfs travel by car to Italy.

Adolf Hitler becomes chancellor of Germany, establishing the totalitarian dictatorship of his National Socialist (Nazi) Party.

T. S. Eliot, *The Use of Poetry and the Use of Criticism;* George Orwell, *Down and Out in Paris and London;* Gertrude Stein, *The Autobiography of Alice B. Toklas;* Nathanael West, *Miss Lonelyhearts;* W. B. Yeats, *The Collected Poems.*

1934   Woolf meets W. B. Yeats at Ottoline Morrell's house. Writes "Walter Sickert: A Conversation."

George Duckworth dies. Roger Fry dies.

Samuel Beckett, *More Pricks Than Kicks;* Nancy Cunard, ed., *Negro: An Anthology;* F. Scott Fitzgerald, *Tender Is the Night;* Wyndham Lewis, *Men Without Art;* Henry Miller, *Tropic of Cancer;* Ezra Pound, *ABC of Reading;* Evelyn Waugh, *A Handful of Dust.*

1935   The Woolfs travel to Germany, where they accidentally get caught up in a parade for Göring. They return to England via Italy and France.

1936   Woolf reads "Am I a Snob?" to the Memoir Club, and publishes "Why Art Today Follows Politics" in the *Daily Worker.*
        Death of George V, who is succeeded by Edward VIII, who then abdicates to marry Wallis Simpson. George VI becomes king. Spanish Civil War (1936–38) begins when General Franco, assisted by Germany and Italy, attacks the Republican government. BBC television begins.
        Djuna Barnes, *Nightwood;* Charlie Chaplin, *Modern Times* (film); Aldous Huxley, *Eyeless in Gaza;* J. M. Keynes, *The General Theory of Employment, Interest and Money;* Rose Macaulay, *Personal Pleasures;* Margaret Mitchell, *Gone with the Wind.*

1937   *The Years* published. Woolf's nephew Julian Bell killed in the Spanish Civil War.
        Neville Chamberlain becomes prime minister.
        Zora Neale Hurston, *Their Eyes Were Watching God;* David Jones, *In Parenthesis;* Pablo Picasso, *Guernica;* John Steinbeck, *Of Mice and Men;* J. R. R. Tolkien, *The Hobbit.*

1938   *Three Guineas* published.
        Germany annexes Austria. Chamberlain negotiates the Munich Agreement ("Peace in our time"), ceding Czech territory to Hitler.
        Samuel Beckett, *Murphy;* Elizabeth Bowen, *The Death of the Heart;* Jean-Paul Sartre, *La Nausée.*

1939   The Woolfs visit Sigmund Freud, living in exile in London having fled the Nazis. They move to Mecklenburgh Square.

Germany occupies Czechoslovakia; Italy occupies Albania; Russia makes a nonaggression pact with Germany. Germany invades Poland and war is declared by Britain and France on Germany, September 3. Deaths of W. B. Yeats (b. 1865), Sigmund Freud (b. 1856), and Ford Madox Ford (b. 1873).

James Joyce, *Finnegans Wake;* John Steinbeck, *The Grapes of Wrath;* Nathanael West, *The Day of the Locust.*

1940   *Roger Fry: A Biography* published. "Thoughts on Peace in an Air Raid" in the *New Republic.* Woolf lectures on "The Leaning Tower" to the Workers Educational Association in Brighton.

The Battle of Britain leads to German night bombings of English cities. The Woolfs' house at Mecklenburgh Square is severely damaged, as is their former house at Tavistock Square. Hogarth Press is moved out of London.

Ernest Hemingway, *For Whom the Bell Tolls;* Christina Stead, *The Man Who Loved Children.*

1941   Woolf drowns herself, March 28, in the River Ouse in Sussex. *Between the Acts* published in July.

Death of James Joyce (b. 1882).

Rebecca West, *Black Lamb and Grey Falcon.*

INTRODUCTION
BY SUSAN GUBAR

NO PIECE of expository prose could be more luminous or, to use one of Virginia Woolf's favorite adjectives, more incandescent than *A Room of One's Own*. Neither could it be more deceptively simple or transparent, especially for Americans sharing her language but unfamiliar with the academic institutions Woolf satirizes in her opening scenes or the legal and social history she confronts throughout. Its incandescence has everything to do with its sometimes charming, sometimes mystifying allusions—and this holds true now, I suspect, for people from any national background. Not just the abundant quotations from literary and historical books but a plethora of sly references, blatantly borrowed characters, artfully constructed symbols, and dramatic ironies signal Woolf's decision to filter her intellectual ambitions through fictional narration, the "lies" she uses to engage the various economic, psychological, aesthetic, and sexual repercussions of gender, and to do so without boring her audience to distraction. The author of such novels as *The Voyage Out, Night and Day, Jacob's Room, Mrs. Dalloway, To the Lighthouse,* and *Orlando*—all completed and published before *A Room of One's Own*—is very much in evidence here. Even the treatise's stark central claim—that every woman needs a room of her own and five hundred pounds a year—condenses complex materialist arguments through a kind of elegant shorthand in need of deciphering.

Shouldn't we recognize Woolf's characters, her Mary Beton, Mary Seton, and Mary Carmichael, many readers wonder; or who exactly is J—H— glimpsed wandering in the gardens of a women's college? What would be the current equivalent of the five hundred pounds Woolf feels every woman ought to have, and why is the incipient genius Judith Shakespeare buried outside the Elephant and Castle? Is it significant that a story about Chloe liking Olivia leads to the admonition, "Do not start. Do not blush"; and exactly what does it mean that Woolf's narrator fears in one passage that a Sir Chartres Biron hides concealed behind a red curtain and in another that one Sir Archibald Bodkin crouches behind table napkins in a cupboard? Hardly trivial, the answers to such questions help establish the evocative reverberations of what has become a classic—if not *the* touchstone text—in the history of feminism. These sorts of queries also underscore Woolf's substantive inquiries into social justice issues throughout *A Room of One's Own* as well as the quarrels many later critics have had with the text, all of which combine to refute easy solutions to the gender inequalities Woolf addresses or reductive interpretations of the text itself.

To begin to address one of the questions raised by the allusions is to move along a single, tightly drawn thread in the complex web of this text's meanings. J—H—, for example, is hardly an arbitrary visitant in the work: Virginia Woolf, who went to see *Jane Harrison* on her deathbed in April of 1928, knew the personal costs the prominent classical scholar paid for her pioneering membership in the earliest generation of British female academics. A famous teacher, Harrison had to overcome her family's resistance to become the first classicist deploying an anthropological approach to Greek religion, and she did so in an effort to prove the historical existence of matriarchy, as her biographer Sandra Peacock has shown. In a 1928 diary entry, Woolf recalled the seventy-eight-year-old woman looking "exalted, satisfied, exhausted" (*Diary* 3: 180); this perception set the stage for the spectral resurrection performed in *A Room of One's Own* when a bent but formidable J—H— appears in the spring twilight, on the campus of a women's college. Clearly such background information might tie together a string of associations linking Victorian intellectual history and women's professional advancements in the early twentieth century with the matriarchal goddesses of ancient Greece. Does the weather change at the moment of Jane Harrison's posthumous appearance in the first chapter because she studied rituals of seasonal renewal?

Endnotes, of course, cannot elaborate on such resonances, only readers can, but critical annotations supply the information necessary to shape supple interpretive responses, reactions attuned to the specific issues Woolf addressed in this, one of her most admired and influential books. "An allusion," the critic Jane Marcus reminds us, "is not an echo until it rings a bell in the common reader's ear as well" (165). The massive amount of biographical and critical scholarship that Woolf's life and work have received over the past several decades has now made such annotations—as well as their appealing echoes in the ears of common readers—possible.

A classic text, then, but one whose allusiveness allowed Woolf to eschew tendentious didacticism, for throughout her life she found repugnant what she mocked as the loudspeaker voice, which was inhospitable to her temperament. Indeed, it is precisely because she refused to hammer home her points or deliver prescriptions like a doctor would drugs or a pedant rules or a judge pronouncements or a preacher sermons that *A Room of One's Own* evinces a tone many readers find whimsically playful, others cloyingly coy or frustratingly evasive. Woolf herself worried about sounding strident, about being labeled and then rejected as either a feminist or a lesbian by the general reading public and even by her sophisticated circle of acquaintances, as my recounting of her letters and diary entries about *A Room*'s composition will subsequently demonstrate. At a later time in Woolf's life, she retrospectively elaborated on the camouflage of her central strategy to a close friend, the composer Ethel Smyth:

> I forced myself to keep my own figure fictitious; legendary. If I had said, Look here am I uneducated, because my brothers used all the family funds which is the fact—Well theyd have said; she has an axe to grind; and no one would have taken me seriously. (June 8, 1933, *Letters* 5: 195)

Making her "figure fictitious" is precisely what Woolf does when, toward the end of the long opening paragraph of *A Room of One's Own,* she claims, " 'I' is only a convenient term for somebody who has no real being." The fabrication of such an impersonated speaker could disguise personal grievances, putting some distance between the indignant author and her "legendary" persona. In a drafted passage of *A Room* about her revulsion at aggressively masculine authors, Woolf wrote and struck through a telling admission: "~~For I am going to be a coward, I thought, & call it / courtesy. I am not going to say aloud what I think of all this fiction & poetry & criticism,~~" (*Women & Fiction* 149). Courtesies and perhaps cowardice (or—to put it more sympathetically—fears), as well as a wish not to replicate an egotism she deplored in the work of some of her peers, do calibrate the fluent lambency of *A Room of One's Own*'s prose style, though some axes *are* ground, quite a few names named, and even the courteous or cowardly evasions have been taken very seriously during the seventy-five years of its lively shelf life thus far.

Not unlike the crossed-out confessions in the draft—"~~I am going to be a coward. . . . I am not going to say aloud what I~~

~~think~~"—Woolf's deflections and hesitations appear in *A Room of One's Own* as self-critical digressions, exclamatory moments of surprise, broken-off diatribes, contradictory equivocations, and offhand asides. Ellipses frequently mark interruptions, but so do shifts in point of view over the passage of time or amid the interpolation of a scene that brings new angles to light. That the essay's first and last sentences begin with the word "but" marks its author's wish to engage in a fluid series of conversations with her interlocutors and with herself. "But–'but'<were> 'buts' beginning again? What ~~was~~ <did> I mean by it this time," Woolf asks of herself in the draft (*Women & Fiction* 157), as if to draw attention to self-questioning as her modus operandi. We need to understand what the proliferation of the word "but" might signify, to recognize Woolf's "legendary" persona, and to understand why Chloe and Olivia could startle blushes to appear, because *A Room of One's Own,* like Woolf's novels, manifests her interest in the always-altering mind bringing modulating perspectives to the idiosyncratic circumstances it perceives: the motility and mobility of consciousness as one individual experiences walking down the street or looking out the window either as an inheritor of or as an alien in her world, or as both, simultaneously or successively; as one human being broods about and through a maternal role model, or a paternal mentor, or through biological mothers and fathers; as one specimen of humanity thinks as a woman, or as a man, or as a womanly man, a manly woman.

We watch Woolf's narrator changing her feelings, moods, convictions, as we change our own about the complex and multidimensional subjects under discussion. While Woolf's "legendary" persona circles around the frustrations to and satisfactions of achieving autonomy, an individual but also collective struggle for the independence upon which fully realized creativity depends, a portrait of the artist as a maturing woman

emerges. Providing a window into Woolf's own struggles as a
writer, this portrait of the woman artist is so impersonally delin-
eated that it serves as a forgivingly lighted mirror for many of
its readers: not the magnifying glass a number of men have
sought from their female dependents, but a glossy, polished surface in which we can see reflected Virginia Woolf's sometimes
bleak, sometimes bright visions of what women have been and
who we ourselves might become. Perhaps a simple summary of
the letters and diary entries devoted to the genesis of *A Room of
One's Own* and then to its development through various drafts
can best illuminate the biographical paths leading Woolf to this
unprecedented and unparalleled achievement.

THOUGH a decidedly literary and print-conscious text, *A Room
of One's Own* is framed as a spoken lecture from its start ("when
you asked me to speak") to its close ("every speech must end
with a peroration"). This is because it originated out of two
talks given at the university Woolf's brothers had attended with
family funds unavailable to her or her talented sister, the painter
Vanessa Bell. Fictionalized as Fernham in the final manuscript,
Newnham and Girton were schools for women at Cambridge,
where degrees were conferred exclusively on men until 1948,
because the women's colleges were not admitted to full university status. (Oxford began granting women degrees in 1920;
Yale, in 1969.) Whether one lecture was given at both colleges,
or different parts of one long paper, or two different essays remains unclear. Prior to the lectures' approaching deadline,
Woolf's letters hardly bode well for the text she was preparing:
The paper at which she labored begins "to shadow even the
downs with its dullness," is "the last I shall ever read in this
hemisphere or the next," for "I can't bear lecturing; it takes ages;
and I do it vilely"; and (this between the two events) "Damn

Girton and speeches" (*Letters* 3: 516, mid-August 1928; 3: 543, October 7, 1928; 3: 551, October 25, 1928).

Despite such jitters, Virginia Woolf—along with her husband, Leonard Woolf, Vanessa, and Vanessa's daughter, Angelica—drove from London to Cambridge on Saturday, October 20, 1928, where she dined at Newnham College and lectured under the auspices of the Newnham Arts Society. The next day she lunched with a fellow of King's College and a number of people associated with Bloomsbury, the circle of bohemian thinkers and artists that formed her intellectual community: George Rylands, Lytton Strachey, John Maynard Keynes, and possibly E. M. Forster. These meals, reversed in chronology, became food for thought in the opening chapter of *A Room of One's Own*. While she gave the first lecture attended by her immediate family, it was her lover, Vita Sackville-West, who on October 26 accompanied Woolf on the train back to Cambridge, this time to Girton College, where she spoke under the auspices of Odtaa, a student society (whose acronym stands for "one damn thing after another").

Of the few attendees who could recall the events later, one student remembered being rather chagrined that the famous author commented on how "beautifully dressed" the "young ladies" were, while another admitted that the dark hall and Woolf's "mellifluous" reading voice caused her to sleep "right through it" (Lee 556–57). In her diary, the forty-six-year-old Woolf recorded her complicated sense of sympathy for, but also alienation from, her audience:

> Starved but valiant young women—that's my impression. Intelligent eager, poor; & destined to become schoolmistresses in shoals. I blandly told them to drink wine & have a room of their own Why should all the splendour,

all the luxury of life be lavished on the Julians & the Fran-
cises, & none on the Phares & the Thomases?. . . . I fancy
sometimes the world changes. I think I see reason spread-
ing. But I should have liked a closer & thicker knowledge
of life. . . . I felt elderly & mature. And nobody respected
me. They were very eager, egotistical, or rather not much
impressed by age & repute. Very little reverence or that
sort of thing about. (October 27, 1928; *Diary* 3: 200–201)

Why were female students like Elsie Elizabeth Phare and Margaret Ellen Thomas, just as deserving as her nephew Julian, denied the amenities he enjoyed?

But also, why did Woolf, the established novelist, feel that
"nobody respected" her? Older and probably better off finan-
cially than most of the students, Woolf had previous experience
as a teacher: She had volunteered at Morley College, a night
school for working men and women, and for almost two years
taught (without pay) composition and history classes. As a
pupil, too, she had received private instruction, most produc-
tively in Greek from her tutor Janet Case. Yet well might she
have felt unimposing to the "starved but valiant" undergradu-
ates afforded precisely the "closer & thicker knowledge" she
had been denied. Though born into a well-to-do and literate
family—her father was a distinguished philosopher, editor, and
biographer; her mother, the author of a book on nursing and
socially conversant with a constellation of London luminaries—
Virginia Woolf would always resent the familial and historical
circumstances dictating that she, like so many daughters of men
prominent in the nineteenth century, was to be denied access to
a university education.

From its opening academic scenes, *A Room of One's Own*
measures the effects of women's exclusion from higher institutions of knowledge, asking whether it has been worse for

women to be shut out of such institutions (and thus shut up) or for men to be shut in. As do a number of short stories by Woolf, many of *A Room*'s subsequent passages, in which the narrator pursues her research by consulting the historians or pulling poems and novels off shelves, meditate on the privations but also, paradoxically, on the privileges of female homeschooling. About the privations of exclusion, she asks, how can a group of people systematically miseducated or uneducated possibly contribute to the ongoing work of the sciences, arts, and humanities and thus to the future evolution of what constitutes Western culture? About the privileges of exclusion, she wonders, do the ingrown eccentricities of elitism, the vanity bred by inordinate wealth, and the competition within universities (as well as the professions they certify) inculcate values so inimical to men's well-being, and to the peace and well-being of the world, that women are lucky to be exempted?

Several months after the lectures at Cambridge and as she lay in bed during a period of illness, Woolf experienced an excited outburst of creativity that led to the drafting in a single month of the first extant version of *A Room of One's Own,* entitled *Women & Fiction.* According to S. P. Rosenbaum, who meticulously transcribed and edited this manuscript for its first publication in 1992, the draft was composed so quickly, at such speed, that the scrawl of Woolf's handwriting made it extremely difficult to decipher. She herself felt she had "made it up at such a rate that when I got pen & paper I was like a water bottle turned upside down. The writing was as quick as my hand could write; too quick, for I am now toiling to revise; but this way gives one freedom & lets one leap from back to back of one's thoughts" (April 1929, *Diary* 3: 222). Taken together, its "considerable conviction" and its form, "half talk half soliloquy allow[ing] me to get more onto the page than any how else," inspired confidence about successful sales (April 1929, *Diary* 3: 221).

Based on the Cambridge talks, the drafty *Women & Fiction* lets us watch Woolf cutting and inserting, stopping and starting, reworking scenes over and over again with various phrasings, as she introduces many of the motifs that found their way into the finalized text, but also as she includes fascinating passages that were ultimately excised. So, for example, when a cat without a tail is mentioned in the draft, its sighting leads to a remark about "some fluke" of the mind "which I leave to Freud to . . . explain" (14). The joke about Sigmund Freud's notion of "female castration" (or its corollary, "penis envy") comes through loud and clear. Has angry Professor X (he has no "von" here) a wife who "twitted him for being such a great lout of a man," or had he simply "failed to get some post in the university" (45)? His superiority complex instantly seems compensatory, a threadbare security blanket. In another excised passage, were "a tribe of women discovered in Central Asia" to have written a play "better than *Lear*" or to have made a discovery of greater "importance than Einsteins," we are informed, public incredulity would turn into rage, rage into the altering of documents, a substitution "for the Jane or Anne on the title page" of a "William or George" (56). Is the absence of the female genius from the past a fact, or has someone tampered with the evidence?

Originally, according to the draft, Shakespeare's sister was given his mother's name, Mary Arden, and "Once she went gallivanting off in the woods dressed like a man" (73–74). Not only the figure of Shakespeare but also the cross-dressing girl might be spin-offs from the novel Woolf completed directly before beginning *A Room,* her biography of *Orlando* (1928). What Chloe, who liked Olivia, shared cannot be immediately detected because the pages of the book "had stuck" together, causing a "fumbling" that leaves time for upsetting visions to flash in the narrator's mind: "the Magistrate coming in . . . the verdict; this book is ~~called~~ obscene; & flames rising, perhaps on Tower Hill, as they consumed <that> masses of ~~print~~ paper" (114). In the wake of the 1928 banning of Radclyffe Hall's *The Well of Loneliness,* a novel about a mannish lesbian "invert" (a male psyche trapped within a female body), Woolf translates obscenity trials into book burnings. When a culture is dominated by the virile sex-consciousness of literary men like "Mr A. & Mr B & Mr C. & Mr D.," it is said to be infected by "Cock-a-doodling" (148, 162). Such crowing alphabet men conjure *To the Lighthouse's* would-be philosopher king Mr. Ramsay, who struts about soldiering on from Q to R. Oddly and with some hilarity in the peroration, as Woolf implores women to use the economic freedom of an inheritance to write books, she ends up telling each and every member of her audience "to kill your Aunt" (171)!

What seems exceptionally moving about perusing Woolf's first slapdash romp through what would eventually become the polished book in your hands may be eerily explained near its opening, when Charles Lamb is described as "shocked" by thinking "it possible that any word in *Lycidas* could have been different from what it is." To witness Woolf amending the words in her treatise might seem a sacrilege to some, to others a precious glimpse into a composition process motivated by authorial courtesy or cowardice. When judged to be particularly significant, the drafted but excised injunctions, biting satire, and hallucinatory visions find their way into the endnotes of this edition so they can haunt the refined printed version. Later fragmentary manuscripts, portions of the typescript for *A Room of One's Own,* and an article on "Women and Fiction," published in the March 1929 issue of the *Forum,* contain further resonant variants and emendations, all well worth studying in Rosenbaum's useful sourcebook. In the typescript of *A Room,* for example, a consciousness that combines manly and womanly attributes is not androgynous but "gunandros" (186), and, about her central thesis, the author requests "~~a generous margin for~~

~~symbolism~~   ~~allowing that money stands for the power to~~
~~contemplate, and that a lock on the door means the power to~~
~~think for oneself~~" (192–93).

On November 7, 1929, one year after the lectures, Woolf's
Diary includes her wish to "write a history, say of Newnham or
the women's movement" (*Diary* 3: 203). Conceivably this project reflects her efforts to revise *Women & Fiction,* which contained quite a few references to the founders of the women's
colleges at Cambridge. In any case, half a year after that entry,
the manuscript had been revised, and while Leonard was reading it, she explained her condensing and melding of the facts of
women's history for the common readers she had in mind:

> About W.&F. I am not sure—a brilliant essay?—I dare-
> say; it has much work in it, many opinions boiled down
> into a kind of jelly, which I have stained red as far as I can.
> But I am eager to be off—to write without any boundary
> coming slick in ones eyes: here my public has been too
> close: facts; getting them malleable, easily yielding to each
> other. (May 1929, *Diary* 3: 223–24)

Only in June does she use the title by which we know the text
today, referring to the need "to correct A Room of one's own"
(*Diary* 3: 233), which soon sponsors dislike of her own "loose-
ness": "This is partly that I don't think things out first; partly
that I stretch my style to take in crumbs of meaning. But the result is a wobbly & diffusity & breathlessness which I detest"
(*Diary* 3: 235).

Woolf alternated hours of "intense correction" of proofs
with an active social life, with trying to fire and then retain her
cook, Nelly, but also with broodings about the experiment in
fiction that would become *The Waves* (*Diary* 3: 237). On Monday, August 19, she finally exulted in "the blessed fact that for

good or bad I have just set the last correction to Women & Fiction, or a Room of One's Own. I shall never read it again I suppose. Good or bad? Has an uneasy life in it I think: you feel the creature arching its back & galloping on, though as usual much is watery & flimsy & pitched in too high a voice" (241–42). The day before it was published in both England and America, she summed up her anxieties about its reception:

> It makes me suspect that there is a shrill feminine tone in it which my intimate friends will dislike. I forecast, then, that I shall get no criticism, except of the evasive jocular kind . . . that the press will be kind & talk of its charm, & sprightiness; also I shall be attacked for a feminist & hinted at for a sapphist; . . . I am afraid it will not be taken seriously. Mrs. Woolf is so accomplished a writer that all she says makes easy reading . . . [her ellipsis] this very feminine logic . . . [her ellipsis] a book to be put in the hands of girls. . . . It is a trifle, I shall say; so it is, but I wrote it with ardour & conviction. (*Diary* 3: 262).

Quite a few of these predictions would in fact come true during her lifetime. An instant bestseller (probably because of "its charm, & sprightiness"), *A Room of One's Own* sold more than twenty-two thousand copies in the first six months of its appearance, and it has never gone out of print either in the United Kingdom or in the United States. To Woolf, who often used the metaphor of fishing (though she may have been thinking of kite flying or sailing), the unprecedented sales felt "like a line running through ones fingers" (*Diary* 3: 272).

Its original cover in England, created by Vanessa Bell, featured a pale pink dust jacket with childish cursive and lowercase lettering in blue, a color pattern that cannot but bring to mind the instant gender packaging performed on babies upon their emergence from the womb. That the script is blue, the page pink, reinforces Woolf's critique of foregrounded male legibility, backgrounded female illegibility. At the center of this design there is an ovenlike or proscenium-like opening, within which appear two blocks, the smaller resting on the larger: a box upon a pedestal, an abstract neck on shoulders, a tiered wedding cake, the crown on the brim of a hat, or simply building blocks. On top of the two rectangles stands a small square clock. Like the bells and watches that chime and tick throughout Woolf's narratives, this timepiece reflects her fascination with sequentiality and duration: the rapid successiveness of seconds or centuries or of a decade that passes like a single night; those numinous moments of being when time seems to stand still; a sense of the present either plastered, like a pane of tinted glass, onto the past or hurtling, like a racing horse, toward the future.

In accord with the central image of the watch, three October days of activities are recounted in *A Room of One's Own*, though within them seasons curiously come and go, as the narrator pursues her daily round of activities, some of which involve analyses of various stages in national and natural histories. Evolution, in particular women's evolving relationships to men and to one another, is the heart of the matter. Women's time, or women's relationship to time, forms another major concern, whether because of the domestic interruptions that fragment women's creative endeavors or because women at certain periods of history could not own the money they earned or because of a wish to usher in a new millennium of incandescent imaginative energy. With its hands set at ten to two, the clock on the original cover forms a V, which might stand for Virginia, or for Vita, or for Vanessa, or for the victorious *Vita Nuova* a resurrected Judith Shakespeare would commence.

Subsequent paperback covers of *A Room of One's Own* often exhibited more representational paintings from the Postimpressionist period or photographs, featuring a solitary female figure gazing out a window or working at a desk, or simply an interior window giving out to a view of the sky, or a study cluttered with books and framed pictures, or a close-up of the printed page of an open volume (oddly, in one case, a French history of the court of Louis XI with a single key on it). The iconography reflects Woolf's profound absorption with space—public geo-political and institutional spaces, but also private familial and personal spaces—as well as her recurrent attention to books: especially the avalanche of male-authored pamphlets, tracts, plays, and poems propounding female insufficiency that contrast sharply with the letters, poems, and novels women managed to write despite the discouragement they continually faced. Given the protests produced by women of letters, from Christine de Pizan to Mary Wollstonecraft and Margaret Fuller, *A Room of One's Own* cannot be judged the first feminist polemic; however, heralding her own subsequent *Three Guineas* (1938) as well as Simone de Beauvoir's *The Second Sex* (1949), it has often been viewed as ushering in the second wave of publications that would follow Betty Friedan's *The Feminine Mystique* (1963) and Kate Millett's *Sexual Politics* (1970), for, as Woolf so often reminded herself and her readers, books do in fact continue each other.

BEYOND THE circumstances of composition that shaped Woolf's brilliance as a prose stylist, the singularity of *A Room of One's Own* derives from the historical moment out of which it originated. Written one decade after women gained the vote in 1918 (1919 in the United States), *A Room of One's Own* contemplates the backlash this political victory launched, specifically the defensive reaction that escalated into the "sex wars" (sometimes called "sex discord" or "sex antagonism") many of her contemporaries fanned or decried during the years following

the Great War. With the franchise won, and with women having made gains in property, educational, professional, and divorce rights, too, many people reacted with fear and anger to the
erosion of men's monopoly over the public sphere. At the same
time, a number of feminists—both male and female—knew
that the vote alone could not be counted upon to right all the
wrongs of the past. "Woolf's particular contribution to the
women's movement," Alex Zwerdling has explained, "was to re-
store a sense of the complexity of the issues after the radical
simplification that had seemed necessary for political action"
(217). Those complexities arose from the economic, psychological, aesthetic, and sexual factors so resonantly explored
throughout the pages of her six chapters. Of course each of
these factors played major roles in Woolf's life, amply described
by a number of biographers and most brilliantly by one of the
most recent, Hermione Lee. What money, psyche, art, and sex
mean in the life helps explain what they might signify in the
work, and (of course) vice versa.

Published on the eve of a worldwide depression, *A Room of
One's Own* places economics at the center of its analysis, so much
so that Woolf worries in her peroration that readers will think
she has "made too much of the importance of material things."
Her narrator, who in due course receives a legacy from an aunt
of five hundred pounds a year, deems it more important than
the granting of the vote. Perhaps this is the case because of the
feminization of poverty Woolf examines as a consequence of
maternity, or the social institutions to which maternity had
given rise, as well as the long legal history that denied married
women the right to own their own property. Elsewhere, not a
legacy but a salary is what Woolf urges women to seek. The
necessity of having sufficient funds for a healthy sense of autonomy, the dependency of intellectual integrity on financial
freedom, the moral quagmire of wanting more money than one

really needs: these themes reflect a definitive change in Woolf's personal situation at the time of *A Room*'s appearance. After the Cambridge lectures and before its publication, Woolf recorded a newfound sense of security: "For the first time since I married 1912—1928—16 years—I have been spending money. The spending muscle does not work naturally yet" (*Diary* 3: 212). Hermione Lee explains about Woolf that "*A Room of One's Own* could be read as her own disguised economic autobiography": At this moment in her life, Woolf had sufficient money to plan, build, and furnish a new room at Monk's House in Sussex (548).

Until 1928 Woolf's income had derived from her husband's investments of their joint capital and from journalism, the reviews and essays (published in the *Times Literary Supplement,* the *Nation,* and the *New Statesman*) that continued to bring in more money than her books. She brought to her marriage with the man she termed "a penniless Jew" more than he had to invest (Lee 320–21); however, like her father before her, she often suffered anxiety attacks over incessant worries about bankruptcy, especially when expenses escalated because of her illnesses. Lee records a sudden jump in 1928, when "her income from books was £1434 (£556 earned in England, £878 in the U.S.A.) and her total income was £1540. Her richest year (total income £2936) was 1929" (Lee 550), the point in time when she and Leonard determined to buy the rights to her earlier novels and bring out a "Uniform Edition" from the Hogarth Press (which they owned and managed together). According to Lee's 1996 biography, the five hundred pounds Woolf feels women should be able to earn annually would be "the equivalent now of an average middle-class salary, about £25,000" (549).

Equivalencies are famously difficult to establish, given permutations in living standards, costs of living, inflation, income taxes, average earnings, not to mention the fluctuating exchange rate. So one can only hazard a guess that in America today the ballpark figure would be something in the order of $37,000, an annual income that might seem weirdly extravagant, absurdly low, or right on target to people coming from various vocational backgrounds and geographical environs. In any case, when twenty years earlier Woolf's own aunt Caroline Emelia Stephen had bequeathed £2,500 to her, but only £100 each to her sister, Vanessa, and her brother Adrian, she had wanted to share her portion, although Quentin Bell doubted that she was successful in doing so (2: 39). Still, this wish for an equality of shares dovetails with one of the most ferocious diatribes in *A Room of One's Own,* which targets "the instinct for possession, the rage for acquisition" driving those in its thrall "to desire other people's fields and goods perpetually; to make frontiers and flags; battleships and poison gas; to offer up their own lives and their children's lives." In our own era of perpetual warfare and acquisition, Woolf's treatise offers a stringent inoculation against rampant consumerism and aggression.

Woolf's fulmination against "the instinct for possession, the rage for acquisition" appears in a passage devoted to her analysis of Professor von X's anger as well as his superiority complex. It thus stands with her subsequent diagnoses of the psychosis of fascism, all clearly influenced by her readings in psychoanalysis; in 1924 the Hogarth Press began publication of the International Psycho-Analytical Library (and after Woolf's death the Press printed in twenty-four volumes James Strachey's translation of the *Standard Edition of the Complete Works of Freud*). Psychology is also brought to bear on particular historical epochs, when certain unconscious tunes cease to hum behind the buzz of conversation, and, of course, on women, specifically in her probing of not only the causes but also the consequences of misogyny. How is self-confidence undermined, she repeatedly asks, by interdictions against female intellectual ambition? Does genius devolve into a pathology when women are informed that it makes them anomalous or aberrant? Indeed, the psychology of creativity forms the central core of her genealogical thinking about the differences between male and female artistry. Under what circumstances, she wants to know, does incandescent creativity become deformed by self-destructive humility or bitterness? How do mothers and fathers, or maternal and paternal precursors, inhibit or promote the success of their descendants? Here, too, biography provides some fascinating background on Woolf's insights into the family's effect on early childhood development.

The route Woolf took toward grappling with the family romance (which Freud viewed as formative in each individual's progress) was the quickest and most treacherous, for she was propelled toward it by traumatic personal experiences that contributed to a succession of disabling breakdowns, as well as her perpetual apprehension about them. She admired the literary acumen of her father; however, Leslie Stephen's self-absorption had tyrannized the entire family, especially Woolf's adored mother, whose death in 1895 plunged the thirteen-year-old into her first bout of mental illness. But a sequence of tragedies involving her siblings also contributed to periodic fugues of confusion and despair: the dimly recalled sexual abuse by her half brothers; the death of a beloved half sister within two years of her mother's death; the sudden illness and death of her favorite brother when Woolf was twenty-four. These traumas led to a condition diagnosed by later scholars as depression, insomnia, anorexia, manic depression, or bipolar disorder. All these terms have been used, along with incest survivor, to explain some of the physical and mental symptoms she frequently suffered: a racing pulse, headaches, fear of people, hearing obscene voices, recurrent fevers, an inexplicable sense of guilt leading to thoughts of suicide. At twenty-nine years of age, just on the brink of a career that would eventually make her a renowned pioneer in

literary modernism, Woolf viewed herself as "a failure—childless—insane too, no writer" (*Letters* 1: 465). Hallucinatory and
suicidal characters populate her subsequent fiction, along with
often conspicuously inept and fatuous physicians, overbearing
fathers, and beautiful but doomed or uncomprehending mothers; by creating such characters, she sometimes believed that
she could function as her own psychoanalyst. In *A Room of
One's Own,* she diagnosed not only her own deeply felt emotions but those of generations of middle-class women sickened
by social circumstances inducing insecurity, self-censorship,
anger, madness.

But perhaps Woolf's psychological symptoms—their intensification of her sense of interiority as well as her anxiety that
this intensified interiority would isolate her from quotidian reality—also help explain the emphasis throughout *A Room of One's
Own* on the importance of aesthetics: the talent or gift that it is
death to hide, the integrity of the work of art, the transforma-
tive capacities of the imaginative faculty in readers and in writers. As in a hallucinatory illness, the novel or poem proposes
something like life that is not life, Woolf reminds us; but art also
serves as an antidote to sickness, for the novel or poem com-
bats a vertiginous sense of unreality often accompanying mental collapse. Although she has been roundly attacked for her
emphasis on the transcendental genius (to some a masculine
concept) and on the struggles of women writers (to some a
class- and race-privileged group), she illuminates in one section
of the conclusion to *Women & Fiction* her almost spiritual faith
in the redemptive qualities of great works of art.

The passage below—note the editor's scrupulous reproduc-
tion of each line break, insertion, and deletion—hints that the
sort of consciousness Woolf associated with aesthetic creativity
amounts to a hyperawareness of the real in an everyday realm always teetering on the brink of muted and thus stifling unreality:

we live in a world

which is wholly real, but very largely muffled up. <for some

    reason almost entirely covered up.>

wh. is half covered up. & from wh. the cloak must be torn

Reality <~~Moreover~~> ~~is a most curious thing, because it is never the~~

~~same for t.~~

(Forgive me for my clumsy use of language) is the thing that

leaps out on us ~~in~~ unexpectedly at some corner. It is the

strangest thing, because one can never foretell when it will

come — {why, for example, a paper drifting along a dirty

street is suddenly real & all the } & it is always different

for different people. Yet it is the quality that ~~gives~~ <alone has

    power>

~~importance~~ to give importance, & lastingness; <leap upon the

    moment & endow it with immediacy> which is

all the stranger, considering what trifles sometimes seem

real, & what mountains mere sawdust. However

this may be, the writer is ~~the expert~~ ~~in touch with~~

~~reality:~~ <a> the lightning conductor ~~whose gift it is~~ to

attract ~~the lasting, the real out of the great mountain of~~

~~that mass of~~ a person whose has ~~the astonishing~~

good fortune to live, more than other people, in the heart of

~~reality.~~ So at least I assume from reading

~~the~~ what are called masterpieces. (*Women & Fiction* 169–70)

The artist as "lightning conductor" has the capacity to feel the
shock of electricity and convey it without being consumed by it.
This stunning bolt of the real slivers the woolly membrane, shat-
ters the suffocating, blanketed, or drugged torpor ordinarily coat-
ing and numbing us from a realization of the immediacy of our
experiences. Both in her fictional characters and in her own life,
a perilous onset of trepidation occurs when "mountains [seem]
mere sawdust." In this context, the supposition in a memoir

"that the shock-receiving capacity is what makes me a writer" elucidates how and why writing became curative for her (*Moments of Being* 72).

Woolf's skepticism about conventional religion and about the conventional disciplines, especially the medical sciences, contrasts with her mystical belief in the healing powers not so much of the artist as a person but of the musical or linguistic or visual composition forged out of enmity at abiding in a world "very largely muffled up." Aestheticism—far from being an elitist retreat—is an anodyne to anaesthetization, a defibrillator to the comatose. Woolf places the aesthetic at the center of her discussion of women's issues not simply to evaluate the historical factors that impeded female writers in the past; not simply to criticize evaluative criteria that privilege the subjects, styles, and genres mined by men over those crafted by women; but also to suggest the enduring vital influence of novels, plays, and poems on their present and future audiences. After a sudden shock or injury, "a revelation of some order" arises by virtue of words that "take away the pain," producing in its place "rapture" (*Moments of Being* 72). Because "behind the cotton wool is hidden a pattern" to which all human beings are connected, she asserts somewhat enigmatically about the rapture of artistry, "There is no Shakespeare; there is no Beethoven; certainly and emphatically there is no God; we are the words; we are the music; we are the thing itself" (*Moments of Being* 72).

How does this mystical affirmation of art inform Virginia Woolf's approach to sexuality and to the much discussed ideal of androgyny? When Woolf came to write the fictional biography of an artist, she pointedly gave her subject an eternal and transsexual life, as if to connect her faith in the immortality of art with her belief in a polymorphous eroticism. *Orlando,* the fantasy produced directly before *A Room of One's Own* and often linked to it, traces the life and work of its eponymous poet from his adolescence in the sixteenth century to her maturation in the twentieth century, a trajectory that makes him/her the quintessence of English literary history. As many immediately noticed, in the character of Orlando, Virginia Woolf had thinly fictionalized Vita Sackville-West, granting her the ancestral house, Knole, her uncle inherited because of laws of entail founded upon the principle of primogeniture. About the character based on her lover, Woolf seems to say, there is no Vita Sackville-West; we are the words; we the music; we the thing itself. A creature first male, then female, and thus one who avoids male-or-female to attain a male-and-female self-sufficiency, the hero/heroine's name seems like a whimsically erotic wish, to be ecstatically "Or-And, Oh!" Such a desire relates to a proposition explored by so-called sexologists like Edward Carpenter and Havelock Ellis at the end of the nineteenth and beginning of the twentieth centuries that, as the novel's narrator puts it, "Different though the sexes are, they intermix" (189). Particularly toward the conclusion of *A Room of One's Own,* this idea results in a meditation on androgyny, though throughout Woolf could be said to be grappling with issues of sexuality prompted by the authoring of the transsexual Orlando and the love affair with Vita Sackville-West, whose BBC broadcast on new books praised the feminine fantasy and masculine authority of *A Room of One's Own.*

Yet where and how Woolf positioned herself on the fraught subject of sex remains under dispute, with some readers understanding *A Room* as an espousal of bisexuality or lesbianism, some interpreting it as a renunciation of sexuality altogether, and still others finding in it an implicit defense of heterosexuality. To those attentive to the famous "Chloe likes Olivia" passage, as well as the network of allusions to Radclyffe Hall's lesbian classic, *The Well of Loneliness,* Woolf seems to be juxtaposing against her critique of male sexuality the alternative and more joyously unplotted erotic relationships women have with other women, or that manly women have with equally androgynous partners. To those attuned to the dead mothers in the text and thus to the fatality of maternity, Woolf appears to be rejecting sexuality, and her satiric portraits of male homosexuality and of masculine virility have been viewed as part and parcel of this rejection. To those who note that the imagery of androgyny revolves around nuptials—a marriage of true minds admitting no impediment, a consummation between complementary masculine and feminine features, the joining of a man and a woman in a taxi—the lyrical solution proposed in *A Room* looks like an ideal related to an effort throughout to transcend the partiality and competition of binary terms (like male and female) so as to arrive at liberating moments of resonant being available to men as well as women.

Many other subjects in *A Room of One's Own* have also issued in contradictory beliefs about Woolf's meaning, held by feminists and antifeminists alike. For example, while Woolf has been attacked as too angry in her caricaturing of men, she has concomitantly been chastened for being fearful of rage, put off by the all too justifiable rancor of her female predecessors. Similarly, she has been denounced both for inflating and for demeaning women's cultural achievements. Although praised as a quasi-Marxist in her materialism, she has been trounced for an elitism inculcated by her relatively privileged background. Heralded as an anti-imperialist, critical of England and Empire (with all its embarrassing capital letters), she nevertheless has been taken to task as a racist, unconscious of her biases about third-world societies and people of color. Perhaps because of the multiple ambiguities of her allusive text, Woolf has also been adopted as a muse by conservatives hostile to the contemporary women's movement and by feminists who share a passionate commitment to women's well-being but whose differences of opinion about sex and gender extend to disagreements over the values, tactics, means, and ends that ought to govern the women's movement.

Curious contradictions or paradoxes (depending on your point of view) proliferate throughout *A Room of One's Own*—about sex-consciousness, the relationship between gender and genre, physiology and language, the need to attain equality or maintain the differences between the sexes—making it possible for Woolf to be quoted and invoked by people with diametrically opposed views. Perhaps for this reason, a number of her aphorisms—"we think back through our mothers if we are women"; "the book has somehow to be adapted to the body"—have functioned less as logical arguments, more as axioms or mantras, Zen-like koans. Through the imaginative exertions of countless revisionary readers who became writers because of and through *A Room of One's Own,* its title has morphed into "a desire of one's own," "one child of one's own," "a womb of one's own," "a tomb of one's own," "a tune of one's own," "no room of one's own," "a literature of their own," "a poetics of our own," and Googling produces some 26,400 sites on the Internet with entries like "A Library of One's Own," "A West Side Apartment of One's Own," "A Room of One's Clone." Although in light of women's recent economic and professional advancements, some will doubtlessly approach Woolf's text as a historical period piece, others continue to register the urgency of its exhortations in their present lives.

As if she intuited its hold on her readers' affections, Woolf herself employed *A Room* as an entry for subsequent returns to its subject, first in a speech entitled "Professions for Women," where she opened by explaining to her audience that "the room is your own but it is still bare," and later in a book that she had begun as a sequel but that, she quickly realized, had become a more controversial pacifist manifesto; in 1938 the Hogarth Press distributed thousands of cards that affixed to favorable reviews of *Three Guineas* a blurb: "The author of A ROOM OF ONE'S OWN asks what can a woman do to prevent war?" (Black 148). Whether through her exertions within her own career or through her readers' elaborations decades after it, such protean textuality is of course her triumph. For there is no Virginia Woolf, one might be led to conclude while turning the pages of this, her most beloved essay, and even no single *Room of One's Own:* Her genius resides in allowing each of her readers to feel that we are the words, we the music, we the thing itself.

WORKS CITED

Bell, Quentin. *Virginia Woolf: A Biography.* 2 vols. New York: Harcourt Brace Jovanovich, 1972.

Black, Naomi. *Virginia Woolf as Feminist.* Ithaca, NY: Cornell University Press, 2004.

Lee, Hermione. *Virginia Woolf.* New York: Vintage Books, 1996.

Marcus, Jane. *Virginia Woolf and the Languages of Patriarchy.* Bloomington: Indiana University Press, 1987.

Peacock, Sandra J. *Jane Ellen Harrison: The Mask and the Self.* New Haven, CT: Yale University Press, 1988.

Woolf, Virginia. *The Diary of Virginia Woolf.* Edited by Anne Olivier Bell, assisted by Andrew McNeillie. Vol. 3 (1925–30). New York: Harcourt Brace Jovanovich, 1980.

———. *The Letters of Virginia Woolf.* Edited by Nigel Nicolson and Joanne Trautmann. 6 vols. New York: Harcourt Brace Jovanovich, 1975–80.

———. *Moments of Being.* Edited by Jeanne Schulkind. New York: Harcourt, 1985.

———. *Orlando.* New York: Harcourt, 1956. Originally published in 1928.

———. "Professions for Women." In *Norton Anthology of Literature by Women,* 2nd edition. Edited by Sandra M. Gilbert and Susan Gubar, 1345–48. New York: W. W. Norton, 1996.

————. *Women & Fiction: The Manuscript Versions of* A Room Of One's Own. Edited by S. P. Rosenbaum. Oxford: Shakespeare Head Press/Blackwell, 1992.
Zwerdling, Alex. *Virginia Woolf and the Real World.* Berkeley: University of California Press, 1986.

———— /

This essay and the annotations of Woolf's text have profited from Sandra M. Gilbert's extensive writings on Virginia Woolf, from the outstanding research assistance of Jamie Horrocks and Julie Wise, and from the smart suggestions of Judith Brown, Edward Comentale, Don Gray, Bonnie Kime Scott, and Mark Hussey.

A Room of One's Own

A Room of One's Own*

CHAPTER ONE

BUT, YOU MAY say, we asked you to speak about women and
fiction—what has that got to do with a room of one's own? I
will try to explain. When you asked me to speak about women
and fiction I sat down on the banks of a river and began to wonder what the words meant. They might mean simply a few remarks about Fanny Burney; a few more about Jane Austen; a
tribute to the Brontës and a sketch of Haworth Parsonage under
snow; some witticisms if possible about Miss Mitford; a respect-
ful allusion to George Eliot; a reference to Mrs. Gaskell and one
would have done. But at second sight the words seemed not so
simple. The title women and fiction might mean, and you may
have meant it to mean, women and what they are like; or it
might mean women and the fiction that they write; or it might
mean women and the fiction that is written about them; or it
might mean that somehow all three are inextricably mixed together and you want me to consider them in that light. But
when I began to consider the subject in this last way, which
seemed the most interesting, I soon saw that it had one fatal
drawback. I should never be able to come to a conclusion. I
should never be able to fulfil what is, I understand, the first duty

*This essay is based upon two papers read to the Arts Society at Newnham and the Odtaa at Girton in
October 1928. The papers were too long to be read in full, and have since been altered and expanded.

of a lecturer—to hand you after an hour's discourse a nugget of pure truth to wrap up between the pages of your notebooks and keep on the mantel-piece for ever. All I could do was to offer you an opinion upon one minor point—a woman must have money and a room of her own if she is to write fiction; and that, as you will see, leaves the great problem of the true nature of woman and the true nature of fiction unsolved. I have shirked the duty of coming to a conclusion upon these two questions—women and fiction remain, so far as I am concerned, unsolved problems. But in order to make some amends I am going to do what I can to show you how I arrived at this opinion about the room and the money. I am going to develop in your presence as fully and freely as I can the train of thought which led me to think this. Perhaps if I lay bare the ideas, the prejudices, that lie behind this statement you will find that they have some bearing upon women and some upon fiction. At any rate, when a subject is highly controversial—and any question about sex is that—one cannot hope to tell the truth. One can only show how one came to hold whatever opinion one does hold. One can only give one's audience the chance of drawing their own conclusions as they observe the limitations, the prejudices, the idiosyncrasies of the speaker. Fiction here is likely to contain more truth than fact. Therefore I propose, making use of all the liberties and licences of a novelist, to tell you the story of the two days that preceded my coming here—how, bowed down by the weight of the subject which you have laid upon my shoulders, I pondered it, and made it work in and out of my daily life. I need not say that what I am about to describe has no existence; Oxbridge is an invention; so is Fernham; "I" is only a convenient term for somebody who has no real being. Lies will flow from my lips, but there may perhaps be some truth mixed up with them; it is for you to seek out this truth and to decide whether any part of it is worth keeping. If not, you will of course throw the whole of it into the wastepaper basket and forget all about it.

Here then was I (call me Mary Beton, Mary Seton, Mary Carmichael or by any name you please—it is not a matter of any importance) sitting on the banks of a river a week or two ago in fine October weather, lost in thought. That collar I have spoken of, women and fiction, the need of coming to some conclusion on a subject that raises all sorts of prejudices and passions, bowed my head to the ground. To the right and left bushes of some sort, golden and crimson, glowed with the colour, even it seemed burnt with the heat, of fire. On the further bank the willows wept in perpetual lamentation, their hair about their shoulders. The river reflected whatever it chose of sky and bridge and burning tree, and when the undergraduate had oared his boat through the reflections they closed again, completely, as if he had never been. There one might have sat the clock round lost in thought. Thought—to call it by a prouder name than it deserved—had let its line down into the stream. It swayed, minute after minute, hither and thither among the reflections and the weeds, letting the water lift it and sink it, until—you know the little tug—the sudden conglomeration of an idea at the end of one's line: and then the cautious hauling of it in, and the careful laying of it out? Alas, laid on the grass how small, how insignificant this thought of mine looked; the sort of fish that a good fisherman puts back into the water so that it may grow fatter and be one day worth cooking and eating. I will not trouble you with that thought now, though if you look carefully you may find it for yourselves in the course of what I am going to say.

But however small it was, it had, nevertheless, the mysterious property of its kind—put back into the mind, it became at once very exciting, and important; and as it darted and sank, and flashed hither and thither, set up such a wash and tumult of ideas that it was impossible to sit still. It was thus that I found myself walking with extreme rapidity across a grass plot. Instantly a man's figure rose to intercept me. Nor did I at first understand that the gesticulations of a curious-looking object, in a cut-away coat and evening shirt, were aimed at me. His face expressed horror and indignation. Instinct rather than reason came to my help; he was a Beadle; I was a woman. This was the turf; there was the path. Only the Fellows and Scholars are allowed here; the gravel is the place for me. Such thoughts were the work of a moment. As I regained the path the arms of the Beadle sank, his face assumed its usual repose, and though turf is better walking than gravel, no very great harm was done. The only charge I could bring against the Fellows and Scholars of whatever the college might happen to be was that in protection of their turf, which has been rolled for 300 years in succession, they had sent my little fish into hiding.

What idea it had been that had sent me so audaciously trespassing I could not now remember. The spirit of peace descended like a cloud from heaven, for if the spirit of peace dwells anywhere, it is in the courts and quadrangles of Oxbridge on a fine October morning. Strolling through those colleges past those ancient halls the roughness of the present seemed smoothed away; the body seemed contained in a miraculous glass cabinet through which no sound could penetrate, and the mind, freed from any contact with facts (unless one trespassed on the turf again), was at liberty to settle down upon whatever meditation was in harmony with the moment. As chance would have it, some stray memory of some old essay about revisiting Oxbridge in the long vacation brought Charles Lamb to mind— Saint Charles, said Thackeray, putting a letter of Lamb's to his forehead. Indeed, among all the dead (I give you my thoughts as they came to me), Lamb is one of the most congenial; one to

whom one would have liked to say, Tell me then how you wrote
your essays? For his essays are superior even to Max Beerbohm's, I thought, with all their perfection, because of that wild
flash of imagination, that lightning crack of genius in the middle
of them which leaves them flawed and imperfect, but starred
with poetry. Lamb then came to Oxbridge perhaps a hundred
years ago. Certainly he wrote an essay—the name escapes me—
about the manuscript of one of Milton's poems which he saw
here. It was *Lycidas* perhaps, and Lamb wrote how it shocked
him to think it possible that any word in *Lycidas* could have been
different from what it is. To think of Milton changing the words
in that poem seemed to him a sort of sacrilege. This led me to
remember what I could of *Lycidas* and to amuse myself with
guessing which word it could have been that Milton had altered,
and why. It then occurred to me that the very manuscript itself
which Lamb had looked at was only a few hundred yards away,
so that one could follow Lamb's footsteps across the quadrangle to that famous library where the treasure is kept. Moreover, I recollected, as I put this plan into execution, it is in this
famous library that the manuscript of Thackeray's *Esmond* is
also preserved. The critics often say that *Esmond* is Thackeray's
most perfect novel. But the affectation of the style, with its imitation of the eighteenth century, hampers one, so far as I can
remember; unless indeed the eighteenth-century style was natural to Thackeray—a fact that one might prove by looking at the
manuscript and seeing whether the alterations were for the benefit of the style or of the sense. But then one would have to decide what is style and what is meaning, a question which—but
here I was actually at the door which leads into the library itself.
I must have opened it, for instantly there issued, like a guardian
angel barring the way with a flutter of black gown instead of white
wings, a deprecating, silvery, kindly gentleman, who regretted in

a low voice as he waved me back that ladies are only admitted to the library if accompanied by a Fellow of the College or furnished with a letter of introduction.

That a famous library has been cursed by a woman is a matter of complete indifference to a famous library. Venerable and calm, with all its treasures safe locked within its breast, it sleeps complacently and will, so far as I am concerned, so sleep for ever. Never will I wake those echoes, never will I ask for that hospitality again, I vowed as I descended the steps in anger. Still an hour remained before luncheon, and what was one to do? Stroll on the meadows? sit by the river? Certainly it was a lovely autumn morning; the leaves were fluttering red to the ground; there was no great hardship in doing either. But the sound of music reached my ear. Some service or celebration was going forward. The organ complained magnificently as I passed the chapel door. Even the sorrow of Christianity sounded in that serene air more like the recollection of sorrow than sorrow itself; even the groanings of the ancient organ seemed lapped in peace. I had no wish to enter had I the right, and this time the verger might have stopped me, demanding perhaps my baptismal certificate, or a letter of introduction from the Dean. But the outside of these magnificent buildings is often as beautiful as the inside. Moreover, it was amusing enough to watch the congregation assembling, coming in and going out again, busying themselves at the door of the chapel like bees at the mouth of a hive. Many were in cap and gown; some had tufts of fur on their shoulders; others were wheeled in bath-chairs; others, though not past middle age, seemed creased and crushed into shapes so singular that one was reminded of those giant crabs and crayfish who heave with difficulty across the sand of an aquarium. As I leant against the wall the University indeed seemed a sanctuary in which are preserved rare types which would soon be obsolete if left to fight for existence on the pavement of the Strand. Old stories of old deans and old dons came back to mind, but before I had summoned up courage to whistle—it used to be said that at the sound of a whistle old Professor —— instantly broke into a gallop—the venerable congregation had gone inside. The outside of the chapel remained. As you know, its high domes and pinnacles can be seen, like a sailing-ship always voyaging never arriving, lit up at night and visible for miles, far away across the hills. Once, presumably, this quadrangle with its smooth lawns, its massive buildings and the chapel itself was marsh too, where the grasses waved and the swine rootled. Teams of horses and oxen, I thought, must have hauled the stone in wagons from far countries, and then with infinite labour the grey blocks in whose shade I was now standing were poised in order one on top of another, and then the painters brought their glass for the windows, and the masons were busy for centuries up on that roof with putty and cement, spade and trowel. Every Saturday somebody must have poured gold and silver out of a leathern purse into their ancient fists, for they had their beer and skittles presumably of an evening. An unending stream of gold and silver, I thought, must have flowed into this court perpetually to keep the stones coming and the masons working; to level, to ditch, to dig and to drain. But it was then the age of faith, and money was poured liberally to set these stones on a deep foundation, and when the stones were raised, still more money was poured in from the coffers of kings and queens and great nobles to ensure that hymns should be sung here and scholars taught. Lands were granted; tithes were paid. And when the age of faith was over and the age of reason had come, still the same flow of gold and silver went on; fellowships were founded; lectureships endowed; only the gold and silver flowed now, not from the coffers of the king, but from the chests of merchants and manufacturers, from the purses of men who had made, say, a fortune from industry, and returned, in their wills, a bounteous share of it to endow more chairs, more lectureships, more fellowships in the university where they had learnt their craft. Hence the libraries and laboratories; the observatories; the splendid equipment of costly and delicate instruments which now stands on glass shelves, where centuries ago the grasses waved and the swine rootled. Certainly, as I strolled round the court, the foundation of gold and silver seemed deep enough; the pavement laid solidly over the wild grasses. Men with trays on their heads went busily from staircase to staircase. Gaudy blossoms flowered in window-boxes. The strains of the gramophone blared out from the rooms within. It was impossible not to reflect—the reflection whatever it may have been was cut short. The clock struck. It was time to find one's way to luncheon.

It is a curious fact that novelists have a way of making us believe that luncheon parties are invariably memorable for something very witty that was said, or for something very wise that was done. But they seldom spare a word for what was eaten. It is part of the novelist's convention not to mention soup and salmon and ducklings, as if soup and salmon and ducklings were of no importance whatsoever, as if nobody ever smoked a cigar or drank a glass of wine. Here, however, I shall take the liberty to defy that convention and to tell you that the lunch on this occasion began with soles, sunk in a deep dish, over which the college cook had spread a counterpane of the whitest cream, save that it was branded here and there with brown spots like the spots on the flanks of a doe. After that came the partridges, but if this suggests a couple of bald, brown birds on a plate you are mistaken. The partridges, many and various, came with all their retinue of sauces and salads, the sharp and the sweet, each in its order; their potatoes, thin as coins but not so hard; their sprouts, foliated as rosebuds but more succulent. And no sooner had the roast and its retinue been done with than the silent

serving-man, the Beadle himself perhaps in a milder manifesta-
tion, set before us, wreathed in napkins, a confection which rose
all sugar from the waves. To call it pudding and so relate it to
rice and tapioca would be an insult. Meanwhile the wineglasses
had flushed yellow and flushed crimson; had been emptied; had
been filled. And thus by degrees was lit, halfway down the spine,
which is the seat of the soul, not that hard little electric light
which we call brilliance, as it pops in and out upon our lips, but
the more profound, subtle and subterranean glow, which is the
rich yellow flame of rational intercourse. No need to hurry. No
need to sparkle. No need to be anybody but oneself. We are all
going to heaven and Vandyck is of the company—in other
words, how good life seemed, how sweet its rewards, how trivial this grudge or that grievance, how admirable friendship and
the society of one's kind, as, lighting a good cigarette, one sunk
among the cushions in the window-seat.

If by good luck there had been an ash-tray handy, if one had
not knocked the ash out of the window in default, if things
had been a little different from what they were, one would not
have seen, presumably, a cat without a tail. The sight of that
abrupt and truncated animal padding softly across the quadrangle changed by some fluke of the subconscious intelligence
the emotional light for me. It was as if some one had let fall a
shade. Perhaps the excellent hock was relinquishing its hold. Certainly, as I watched the Manx cat pause in the middle of the lawn
as if it too questioned the universe, something seemed lacking,
something seemed different. But what was lacking, what was different, I asked myself, listening to the talk. And to answer that
question I had to think myself out of the room, back into the
past, before the war indeed, and to set before my eyes the model
of another luncheon party held in rooms not very far distant
from these; but different. Everything was different. Meanwhile
the talk went on among the guests, who were many and young,

some of this sex, some of that; it went on swimmingly, it went on agreeably, freely, amusingly. And as it went on I set it against the background of that other talk, and as I matched the two together I had no doubt that one was the descendant, the legitimate heir of the other. Nothing was changed; nothing was different save only—here I listened with all my ears not entirely to what was being said, but to the murmur or current behind it. Yes, that was it—the change was there. Before the war at a luncheon party like this people would have said precisely the same things but they would have sounded different, because in those days they were accompanied by a sort of humming noise, not articulate, but musical, exciting, which changed the value of the words themselves. Could one set that humming noise to words? Perhaps with the help of the poets one could. A book lay beside me and, opening it, I turned casually enough to Tennyson. And here I found Tennyson was singing:

> There has fallen a splendid tear
>   From the passion-flower at the gate.
> She is coming, my dove, my dear;
>   She is coming, my life, my fate;
> The red rose cries, "She is near, she is near";
>   And the white rose weeps, "She is late";
> The larkspur listens, "I hear, I hear";
>   And the lily whispers, "I wait."

Was that what men hummed at luncheon parties before the war? And the women?

> My heart is like a singing bird
>   Whose nest is in a water'd shoot;
> My heart is like an apple tree

Whose boughs are bent with thick-set fruit;
My heart is like a rainbow shell
    That paddles in a halcyon sea;
My heart is gladder than all these
    Because my love is come to me.

Was that what women hummed at luncheon parties before the war?

There was something so ludicrous in thinking of people humming such things even under their breath at luncheon parties before the war that I burst out laughing, and had to explain my laughter by pointing at the Manx cat, who did look a little absurd, poor beast, without a tail, in the middle of the lawn. Was he really born so, or had he lost his tail in an accident? The tailless cat, though some are said to exist in the Isle of Man, is rarer than one thinks. It is a queer animal, quaint rather than beautiful. It is strange what a difference a tail makes—you know the sort of things one says as a lunch party breaks up and people are finding their coats and hats.

This one, thanks to the hospitality of the host, had lasted far into the afternoon. The beautiful October day was fading and the leaves were falling from the trees in the avenue as I walked through it. Gate after gate seemed to close with gentle finality behind me. Innumerable beadles were fitting innumerable keys into well-oiled locks; the treasure-house was being made secure for another night. After the avenue one comes out upon a road—I forget its name—which leads you, if you take the right turning, along to Fernham. But there was plenty of time. Dinner was not till half-past seven. One could almost do without dinner after such a luncheon. It is strange how a scrap of poetry works in the mind and makes the legs move in time to it along the road. Those words—

There has fallen a splendid tear
   From the passion-flower at the gate.
She is coming, my dove, my dear—

sang in my blood as I stepped quickly along towards Headingley. And then, switching off into the other measure, I sang,
where the waters are churned up by the weir:

   My heart is like a singing bird
      Whose nest is in a water'd shoot;
   My heart is like an apple tree . . .

What poets, I cried aloud, as one does in the dusk, what poets
they were!

In a sort of jealousy, I suppose, for our own age, silly and
absurd though these comparisons are, I went on to wonder if
honestly one could name two living poets now as great as Tennyson and Christina Rossetti were then. Obviously it is impossible, I thought, looking into those foaming waters, to compare
them. The very reason why the poetry excites one to such aban-
donment, such rapture, is that it celebrates some feeling that
one used to have (at luncheon parties before the war perhaps),
so that one responds easily, familiarly, without troubling to
check the feeling, or to compare it with any that one has now.
But the living poets express a feeling that is actually being made
and torn out of us at the moment. One does not recognize it in
the first place; often for some reason one fears it; one watches
it with keenness and compares it jealously and suspiciously with
the old feeling that one knew. Hence the difficulty of modern
poetry; and it is because of this difficulty that one cannot remember more than two consecutive lines of any good modern
poet. For this reason—that my memory failed me—the argument flagged for want of material. But why, I continued, mov-

ing on towards Headingley, have we stopped humming under our breath at luncheon parties? Why has Alfred ceased to sing

> She is coming, my dove, my dear?

Why has Christina ceased to respond

> My heart is gladder than all these
> Because my love is come to me?

Shall we lay the blame on the war? When the guns fired in August 1914, did the faces of men and women show so plain in each other's eyes that romance was killed? Certainly it was a shock (to women in particular with their illusions about education, and so on) to see the faces of our rulers in the light of the shell-fire. So ugly they looked—German, English, French—so stupid. But lay the blame where one will, on whom one will, the illusion which inspired Tennyson and Christina Rossetti to sing so passionately about the coming of their loves is far rarer now than then. One has only to read, to look, to listen, to remember. But why say "blame"? Why, if it was an illusion, not praise the catastrophe, whatever it was, that destroyed illusion and put truth in its place? For truth . . . those dots mark the spot where, in search of truth, I missed the turning up to Fernham. Yes indeed, which was truth and which was illusion, I asked myself. What was the truth about these houses, for example, dim and festive now with their red windows in the dusk, but raw and red and squalid, with their sweets and their boot-laces, at nine o'clock in the morning? And the willows and the river and the gardens that run down to the river, vague now with the mist stealing over them, but gold and red in the sunlight—which was the truth, which was the illusion about them? I spare you the twists and turns of my cogitations, for no conclusion was found on the road to Headingley, and I ask you to suppose that I soon found out my mistake about the turning and retraced my steps to Fernham.

As I have said already that it was an October day, I dare not forfeit your respect and imperil the fair name of fiction by changing the season and describing lilacs hanging over garden walls, crocuses, tulips and other flowers of spring. Fiction must stick to facts, and the truer the facts the better the fiction——so we are told. Therefore it was still autumn and the leaves were still yellow and falling, if anything, a little faster than before, because it was now evening (seven twenty-three to be precise) and a breeze (from the southwest to be exact) had risen. But for all that there was something odd at work:

> My heart is like a singing bird
>> Whose nest is in a water'd shoot;
> My heart is like an apple tree
>> Whose boughs are bent with thick-set fruit—

perhaps the words of Christina Rossetti were partly responsible for the folly of the fancy—it was nothing of course but a fancy—that the lilac was shaking its flowers over the garden walls, and the brimstone butterflies were scudding hither and thither, and the dust of the pollen was in the air. A wind blew, from what quarter I know not, but it lifted the half-grown leaves so that there was a flash of silver grey in the air. It was the time between the lights when colours undergo their intensification and purples and golds burn in window-panes like the beat of an excitable heart; when for some reason the beauty of the world revealed and yet soon to perish (here I pushed into the garden, for, unwisely, the door was left open and no beadles seemed about), the beauty of the world which is so soon to perish, has two edges, one of laughter, one of anguish, cutting the heart asunder. The gardens of Fernham lay before me in the spring twilight, wild and open, and in the long grass, sprinkled and carelessly flung, were daffodils and bluebells, not orderly perhaps at the best of times, and now wind-blown and waving as they tugged at their roots. The windows of the building, curved like ships' windows among generous waves of red brick, changed from lemon to silver under the flight of the quick spring clouds. Somebody was in a hammock, somebody, but in this light they were phantoms only, half guessed, half seen, raced across the grass—would no one stop her?—and then on the terrace, as if popping out to breathe the air, to glance at the garden, came a bent figure, formidable yet humble, with her great forehead and her shabby dress—could it be the famous scholar, could it be J—— H—— herself? All was dim, yet intense too, as if the scarf which the dusk had flung over the garden were torn asunder by star or sword—the flash of some terrible reality leaping, as its way is, out of the heart of the spring. For youth——

Here was my soup. Dinner was being served in the great dining-hall. Far from being spring it was in fact an evening in October. Everybody was assembled in the big dining-room. Dinner was ready. Here was the soup. It was a plain gravy soup. There was nothing to stir the fancy in that. One could have seen through the transparent liquid any pattern that there might have been on the plate itself. But there was no pattern. The plate was plain. Next came beef with its attendant greens and potatoes— a homely trinity, suggesting the rumps of cattle in a muddy market, and sprouts curled and yellowed at the edge, and bargaining and cheapening, and women with string bags on Monday morning. There was no reason to complain of human nature's daily food, seeing that the supply was sufficient and coal-miners doubtless were sitting down to less. Prunes and custard followed. And if any one complains that prunes, even when mitigated by custard, are an uncharitable vegetable (fruit they are not), stringy as a miser's heart and exuding a fluid such as might run in misers' veins who have denied themselves wine and warmth for eighty years and yet not given to the poor, he should reflect that there are people whose charity embraces even the prune. Biscuits and cheese came next, and here the water-jug was liberally passed round, for it is the nature of biscuits to be dry, and these were biscuits to the core. That was all. The meal was over. Everybody scraped their chairs back; the swing-doors swung violently to and fro; soon the hall was emptied of every sign of food and made ready no doubt for breakfast next morning. Down corridors and up staircases the youth of England went banging and singing. And was it for a guest, a stranger (for I had no more right here in Fernham than in Trinity or Somerville or Girton or Newnham or Christchurch), to say, "The dinner was not good," or to say (we were now, Mary Seton and I, in her sitting-room), "Could we not have dined up here alone?" for if I had said anything of the kind I should have been prying and searching into the secret economies of a house which to the stranger wears so fine a front of gaiety and courage. No, one could say nothing of the sort. Indeed, conversation for a moment flagged. The human frame being what it is, heart, body and brain all mixed together, and not contained in separate compartments as they will be no doubt in another million years, a good dinner is of great importance to good talk. One cannot think well, love well, sleep well, if one has not dined well. The lamp in the spine does not light on beef and prunes. We are all *probably* going to heaven, and Vandyck is, we *hope,* to meet us round the next corner—that is the dubious and qualifying state of mind that beef and prunes at the end of the day's work breed between them. Happily my friend, who taught science, had a cupboard where there was a squat bottle and little glasses—(but there should have been sole and partridge to begin with)—so that we were able to draw up to the fire and repair some of the damages of the day's living. In a minute or so we were slipping freely in and out among all those objects of curiosity and interest which form in the mind in the absence of a particular person, and are naturally to be discussed on coming together again—how somebody has married, another has not; one thinks this, another that; one has improved out of all knowledge, the other most amazingly gone to the bad—with all those speculations upon human nature and the character of the amazing world we live in which spring naturally from such beginnings. While these things were being said, however, I became shamefacedly aware of a current setting in of its own accord and carrying everything forward to an end of its own. One might be talking of Spain or Portugal, of book or racehorse, but the real interest of whatever was said was none of those things, but a scene of masons on a high roof some five centuries ago. Kings and nobles brought treasure in huge sacks and poured it under the earth. This scene was for ever coming alive in my mind and placing itself by another of lean cows and a muddy market and withered greens and the stringy hearts of old men—these two pictures, disjointed and disconnected and nonsensical as they were, were for ever coming together and combating each other and had me entirely at their mercy. The best course, unless the whole talk was to be distorted, was to expose what was in my mind to the air, when with good luck it would fade and crumble like the head of the dead king when they opened the coffin at Windsor. Briefly, then, I told Miss Seton about the masons who had been all those years on the roof of the chapel, and about the kings and queens and nobles bearing sacks of gold and silver on their shoulders, which they shovelled into the earth; and then how the great financial magnates of our own time came and laid cheques and bonds, I suppose, where the others had laid ingots and rough lumps of gold. All that lies beneath the colleges down there, I said; but this college, where we are now sitting, what lies beneath its gallant red brick and the wild unkempt grasses of the garden? What force is behind the plain china off which we dined, and (here it popped out of my mouth before I could stop it) the beef, the custard and the prunes?

Well, said Mary Seton, about the year 1860—Oh, but you know the story, she said, bored, I suppose, by the recital. And she told me—rooms were hired. Committees met. Envelopes were addressed. Circulars were drawn up. Meetings were held; letters were read out; so-and-so has promised so much; on the contrary, Mr. —— won't give a penny. The *Saturday Review* has been very rude. How can we raise a fund to pay for offices? Shall we hold a bazaar? Can't we find a pretty girl to sit in the front row? Let us look up what John Stuart Mill said on the subject. Can any one persuade the editor of the —— to print a letter? Can we get Lady —— to sign it? Lady —— is out of town. That was the way it was done, presumably, sixty years ago, and it was a prodigious effort, and a great deal of time was spent on it. And it was only after a long struggle and with the utmost difficulty that they got thirty thousand pounds together.[1] So obviously we cannot have wine and partridges and servants carrying tin dishes on their heads, she said. We cannot have sofas and separate rooms. "The amenities," she said, quoting from some book or other, "will have to wait."[2]

At the thought of all those women working year after year and finding it hard to get two thousand pounds together, and as

---

[1]"We are told that we ought to ask for £30,000 at least. . . . It is not a large sum, considering that there is to be but one college of this sort for Great Britain, Ireland and the Colonies, and considering how easy it is to raise immense sums for boys' schools. But considering how few people really wish women to be educated, it is a good deal."—LADY STEPHEN, *Life of Miss Emily Davies.*

[2]Every penny which could be scraped together was set aside for building, and the amenities had to be postponed.—R. STRACHEY, *The Cause.*

much as they could do to get thirty thousand pounds, we burst out in scorn at the reprehensible poverty of our sex. What had our mothers been doing then that they had no wealth to leave us? Powdering their noses? Looking in at shop windows? Flaunting in the sun at Monte Carlo? There were some photographs on the mantel-piece. Mary's mother—if that was her picture—may have been a wastrel in her spare time (she had thirteen children by a minister of the church), but if so her gay and dissipated life had left too few traces of its pleasures on her face. She was a homely body; an old lady in a plaid shawl which was fastened by a large cameo; and she sat in a basket-chair, encouraging a spaniel to look at the camera, with the amused, yet strained expression of one who is sure that the dog will move directly the bulb is pressed. Now if she had gone into business; had become a manufacturer of artificial silk or a magnate on the Stock Exchange; if she had left two or three hundred thousand pounds to Fernham, we could have been sitting at our ease tonight and the subject of our talk might have been archaeology, botany, anthropology, physics, the nature of the atom, mathematics, astronomy, relativity, geography. If only Mrs. Seton and her mother and her mother before her had learnt the great art of making money and had left their money, like their fathers and their grandfathers before them, to found fellowships and lectureships and prizes and scholarships appropriated to the use of their own sex, we might have dined very tolerably up here alone off a bird and a bottle of wine; we might have looked forward without undue confidence to a pleasant and honourable lifetime spent in the shelter of one of the liberally endowed professions. We might have been exploring or writing; mooning about the venerable places of the earth; sitting contemplative on the steps of the Parthenon, or going at ten to an office and coming home comfortably at half-past four to write a little poetry. Only, if Mrs. Seton and her like had gone into business at the age of fifteen, there would have been—that was the snag in the argument—no Mary. What, I asked, did Mary think of that? There between the curtains was the October night, calm and lovely, with a star or two caught in the yellowing trees. Was she ready to resign her share of it and her memories (for they had been a happy family, though a large one) of games and quarrels up in Scotland, which she is never tired of praising for the fineness of its air and the quality of its cakes, in order that Fernham might have been endowed with fifty thousand pounds or so by a stroke of the pen? For, to endow a college would necessitate the suppression of families altogether. Making a fortune and bearing thirteen children—no human being could stand it. Consider the facts, we said. First there are nine months before the baby is born. Then the baby is born. Then there are three or four months spent in feeding the baby. After the baby is fed there are certainly five years spent in playing with the baby. You cannot, it seems, let children run about the streets. People who have seen them running wild in Russia say that the sight is not a pleasant one. People say, too, that human nature takes its shape in the years between one and five. If Mrs. Seton, I said, had been making money, what sort of memories would you have had of games and quarrels? What would you have known of Scotland, and its fine air and cakes and all the rest of it? But it is useless to ask these questions, because you would never have come into existence at all. Moreover, it is equally useless to ask what might have happened if Mrs. Seton and her mother and her mother before her had amassed great wealth and laid it under the foundations of college and library, because, in the first place, to earn money was impossible for them, and in the second, had it been possible, the law denied them the right to possess what money they earned. It is only for the last forty-eight years that Mrs. Seton has had a penny of her own. For all the centuries before that it would have been her husband's property—a thought which, perhaps, may have had its share in keeping Mrs. Seton and her mothers off the Stock Exchange. Every penny I earn, they may have said, will be taken from me and disposed of according to my husband's wisdom—perhaps to found a scholarship or to endow a fellowship in Balliol or Kings, so that to earn money, even if I could earn money, is not a matter that interests me very greatly. I had better leave it to my husband.

At any rate, whether or not the blame rested on the old lady who was looking at the spaniel, there could be no doubt that for some reason or other our mothers had mismanaged their affairs very gravely. Not a penny could be spared for "amenities"; for partridges and wine, beadles and turf, books and cigars, libraries and leisure. To raise bare walls out of bare earth was the utmost they could do.

So we talked standing at the window and looking, as so many thousands look every night, down on the domes and towers of the famous city beneath us. It was very beautiful, very mysterious in the autumn moonlight. The old stone looked very white and venerable. One thought of all the books that were assembled down there; of the pictures of old prelates and worthies hanging in the panelled rooms; of the painted windows that would be throwing strange globes and crescents on the pavement; of the tablets and memorials and inscriptions; of the fountains and the grass; of the quiet rooms looking across the quiet quadrangles. And (pardon me the thought) I thought, too, of the admirable smoke and drink and the deep armchairs and the pleasant carpets: of the urbanity, the geniality, the dignity which are the offspring of luxury and privacy and space. Certainly our mothers had not provided us with anything comparable to all this—our mothers who found it difficult to scrape together thirty thousand pounds, our mothers who bore thirteen children to ministers of religion at St. Andrews.

So I went back to my inn, and as I walked through the dark
streets I pondered this and that, as one does at the end of the
day's work. I pondered why it was that Mrs. Seton had no
money to leave us; and what effect poverty has on the mind;
and what effect wealth has on the mind; and I thought of the
queer old gentlemen I had seen that morning with tufts of fur
upon their shoulders; and I remembered how if one whistled
one of them ran; and I thought of the organ booming in the
chapel and of the shut doors of the library; and I thought how
unpleasant it is to be locked out; and I thought how it is worse
perhaps to be locked in; and, thinking of the safety and pros-
perity of the one sex and of the poverty and insecurity of the
other and of the effect of tradition and of the lack of tradition
upon the mind of a writer, I thought at last that it was time to
roll up the crumpled skin of the day, with its arguments and its
impressions and its anger and its laughter, and cast it into the
hedge. A thousand stars were flashing across the blue wastes
of the sky. One seemed alone with an inscrutable society. All
human beings were laid asleep—prone, horizontal, dumb. Nobody seemed stirring in the streets of Oxbridge. Even the door
of the hotel sprang open at the touch of an invisible hand—not
a boots was sitting up to light me to bed, it was so late.

CHAPTER TWO

THE SCENE, if I may ask you to follow me, was now changed. The leaves were still falling, but in London now, not Oxbridge; and I must ask you to imagine a room, like many thousands, with a window looking across people's hats and vans and motor-cars to other windows, and on the table inside the room a blank sheet of paper on which was written in large letters WOMEN AND FICTION, but no more. The inevitable sequel to lunching and dining at Oxbridge seemed, unfortunately, to be a visit to the British Museum. One must strain off what was personal and accidental in all these impressions and so reach the pure fluid, the essential oil of truth. For that visit to Oxbridge and the luncheon and the dinner had started a swarm of questions. Why did men drink wine and women water? Why was one sex so prosperous and the other so poor? What effect has poverty on fiction? What conditions are necessary for the creation of works of art?—a thousand questions at once suggested themselves. But one needed answers, not questions; and an answer was only to be had by consulting the learned and the unprejudiced, who have removed themselves above the strife of tongue and the confusion of body and issued the result of their reasoning and research in books which are to be found in the British Museum. If truth is not to be found on the shelves of the British Museum, where, I asked myself, picking up a note-book and a pencil, is truth?

Thus provided, thus confident and enquiring, I set out in the pursuit of truth. The day, though not actually wet, was dismal, and the streets in the neighborhood of the Museum were full of open coal-holes, down which sacks were showering; four-wheeled cabs were drawing up and depositing on the pavement corded boxes containing, presumably, the entire wardrobe of some Swiss or Italian family seeking fortune or refuge or some other desirable commodity which is to be found in the boarding-houses of Bloomsbury in the winter. The usual hoarse-voiced men paraded the streets with plants on barrows. Some shouted; others sang. London was like a workshop. London was like a machine. We were all being shot backwards and forwards on this plain foundation to make some pattern. The British Museum was another department of the factory. The swing-doors swung open; and there one stood under the vast dome, as if one were a thought in the huge bald forehead which is so splendidly encircled by a band of famous names. One went to the counter; one took a slip of paper; one opened a volume of the catalogue, and . . . . . the five dots here indicate five separate minutes of stupefaction, wonder and bewilderment. Have you any notion of how many books are written about women in the course of one year? Have you any notion how many are written by men? Are you aware that you are, perhaps, the most discussed animal in the universe? Here had I come with a notebook and a pencil proposing to spend a morning reading, supposing that at the end of the morning I should have transferred the truth to my notebook. But I should need to be a herd of elephants, I thought, and a wilderness of spiders, desperately referring to the animals that are reputed longest lived and most multitudinously eyed, to cope with all this. I should need claws of steel and beak of brass even to penetrate the husk. How shall I ever find the grains of truth embedded in all this mass of paper, I asked myself, and in despair began running my eye up and down the long list of titles. Even the names of the books gave me food for thought. Sex and its nature might well attract doctors and biologists; but what was surprising and difficult of explanation was the fact that sex—woman, that is to say—also attracts agreeable essayists, light-fingered novelists, young men who have taken the M.A. degree; men who have taken no degree; men who have no apparent qualification save that they are not women. Some of these books were, on the face of it, frivolous and facetious; but many, on the other hand, were serious and prophetic, moral and hortatory. Merely to read the titles suggested innumerable schoolmasters, innumerable clergymen mounting their platforms and pulpits and holding forth with loquacity which far exceeded the hour usually allotted to such discourse on this one subject. It was a most strange phenomenon; and apparently— here I consulted the letter M—one confined to male sex. Women do not write books about men—a fact that I could not help welcoming with relief, for if I had first to read all that men have written about women, then all that women have written about men, the aloe that flowers once in a hundred years would flower twice before I could set pen to paper. So, making a perfectly arbitrary choice of a dozen volumes or so, I sent my slips of paper to lie in the wire tray, and waited in my stall, among the other seekers for the essential oil of truth.

What could be the reason, then, of this curious disparity, I wondered, drawing cart-wheels on the slips of paper provided by the British taxpayer for other purposes. Why are women, judging from this catalogue, so much more interesting to men than men are to women? A very curious fact it seemed, and my mind wandered to picture the lives of men who spend their time in writing books about women; whether they were old or young, married or unmarried, red-nosed or hump-backed—anyhow, it

was flattering, vaguely, to feel oneself the object of such attention, provided that it was not entirely bestowed by the crippled
and the infirm—so I pondered until all such frivolous thoughts
were ended by an avalanche of books sliding down on to the
desk in front of me. Now the trouble began. The student who
has been trained in research at Oxbridge has no doubt some
method of shepherding his question past all distractions till it
runs into its answer as a sheep runs into its pen. The student
by my side, for instance, who was copying assiduously from a
scientific manual was, I felt sure, extracting pure nuggets of the
essential ore every ten minutes or so. His little grunts of satisfaction indicated so much. But if, unfortunately, one has had
no training in a university, the question far from being shep-
herded to its pen flies like a frightened flock hither and thither,
helter-skelter, pursued by a whole pack of hounds. Professors,
schoolmasters, sociologists, clergymen, novelists, essayists, jour-
nalists, men who had no qualification save that they were not
women, chased my simple and single question—Why are women
poor?—until it became fifty questions; until the fifty questions
leapt frantically into mid-stream and were carried away. Every
page in my notebook was scribbled over with notes. To show
the state of mind I was in, I will read you a few of them, explaining that the page was headed quite simply, WOMEN AND
POVERTY, in block letters; but what followed was something
like this:

> Condition in Middle Ages of,
> Habits in the Fiji Islands of,
> Worshipped as goddesses by,
> Weaker in moral sense than,
> Idealism of,
> Greater conscientiousness of,
> South Sea Islanders, age of puberty among,

Attractiveness of,
Offered as sacrifice to,
Small size of brain of,
Profounder sub-consciousness of,
Less hair on the body of,
Mental, moral and physical inferiority of,
Love of children of,
Greater length of life of,
Weaker muscles of,
Strength of affections of,
Vanity of,
Higher education of,
Shakespeare's opinion of,
Lord Birkenhead's opinion of,
Dean Inge's opinion of,
La Bruyère's opinion of,
Dr. Johnson's opinion of,
Mr. Oscar Browning's opinion of, . . .

Here I drew breath and added, indeed, in the margin, Why does Samuel Butler say, "Wise men never say what they think of women"? Wise men never say anything else apparently. But, I continued, leaning back in my chair and looking at the vast dome in which I was a single but by now somewhat harassed thought, what is so unfortunate is that wise men never think the same thing about women. Here is Pope:

Most women have no character at all.

And here is La Bruyère:

Les femmes sont extrêmes; elles sont meilleures ou pires que les hommes—

a direct contradiction by keen observers who were contemporary. Are they capable of education or incapable? Napoleon
thought them incapable. Dr. Johnson thought the opposite.[1]
Have they souls or have they not souls? Some savages say they
have none. Others, on the contrary, maintain that women are
half divine and worship them on that account.[2] Some sages hold
that they are shallower in the brain; others that they are deeper
in the consciousness. Goethe honoured them; Mussolini de-
spises them. Wherever one looked men thought about women
and thought differently. It was impossible to make head or tail
of it all, I decided, glancing with envy at the reader next door
who was making the neatest abstracts, headed often with an A
or a B or a C, while my own notebook rioted with the wildest
scribble of contradictory jottings. It was distressing, it was be-
wildering, it was humiliating. Truth had run through my fingers.
Every drop had escaped.

　　I could not possibly go home, I reflected, and add as a serious contribution to the study of women and fiction that women
have less hair on their bodies than men, or that the age of puberty
among the South Sea Islanders is nine—or is it ninety?—even
the handwriting had become in its distraction indecipherable. It
was disgraceful to have nothing more weighty or respectable
to show after a whole morning's work. And if I could not grasp
the truth about W. (as for brevity's sake I had come to call her)
in the past, why bother about W. in the future? It seemed pure
waste of time to consult all those gentlemen who specialise in

---

[1] "'Men know that women are an overmatch for them, and therefore they choose the weak-
est or the most ignorant. If they did not think so, they never could be afraid of women
knowing as much as themselves.' . . . In justice to the sex, I think it but candid to acknowl-
edge that, in a subsequent conversation, he told me that he was serious in what he said."
—BOSWELL, *The Journal of a Tour to the Hebrides.*

[2] "The ancient Germans believed that there was something holy in women, and accordingly
consulted them as oracles."—FRAZER, *Golden Bough.*

woman and her effect on whatever it may be—politics, children, wages, morality—numerous and learned as they are. One might as well leave their books unopened.

But while I pondered I had unconsciously, in my listlessness, in my desperation, been drawing a picture where I should, like my neighbour, have been writing a conclusion. I had been drawing a face, a figure. It was the face and the figure of Professor von X. engaged in writing his monumental work entitled *The Mental, Moral, and Physical Inferiority of the Female Sex.* He was not in my picture a man attractive to women. He was heavily built; he had a great jowl; to balance that he had very small eyes; he was very red in the face. His expression suggested that he was labouring under some emotion that made him jab his pen on the paper as if he were killing some noxious insect as he wrote, but even when he had killed it that did not satisfy him; he must go on killing it; and even so, some cause for anger and irritation remained. Could it be his wife, I asked, looking at my picture. Was she in love with a cavalry officer? Was the cavalry officer slim and elegant and dressed in astrachan? Had he been laughed at, to adopt the Freudian theory, in his cradle by a pretty girl? For even in his cradle the professor, I thought, could not have been an attractive child. Whatever the reason, the professor was made to look very angry and very ugly in my sketch, as he wrote his great book upon the mental, moral and physical inferiority of women. Drawing pictures was an idle way of finishing an unprofitable morning's work. Yet it is in our idleness, in our dreams, that the submerged truth sometimes comes to the top. A very elementary exercise in psychology, not to be dignified by the name of psycho-analysis, showed me, on looking at my notebook, that the sketch of the angry professor had been made in anger. Anger had snatched my pencil while I dreamt. But what was anger doing there? Interest, confusion, amusement, boredom—all these emotions I could trace and name as they succeeded each other throughout the morning. Had anger, the black snake, been lurking among them? Yes, said the sketch, anger had. It referred me unmistakably to the one book, to the one phrase, which had roused the demon; it was the professor's statement about the mental, moral and physical inferiority of women. My heart had leapt. My cheeks had burnt. I had flushed with anger. There was nothing specially remarkable, however foolish, in that. One does not like to be told that one is naturally the inferior of a little man—I looked at the student next me—who breathes hard, wears a ready-made tie, and has not shaved this fortnight. One has certain foolish vanities. It is only human nature, I reflected, and began drawing cart-wheels and circles over the angry professor's face till he looked like a burning bush or a flaming comet—anyhow, an apparition without human semblance or significance. The professor was nothing now but a faggot burning on the top of Hampstead Heath. Soon my own anger was explained and done with; but curiosity remained. How explain the anger of the professors? Why were they angry? For when it came to analysing the impression left by these books there was always an element of heat. This heat took many forms; it showed itself in satire, in sentiment, in curiosity, in reprobation. But there was another element which was often present and could not immediately be identified. Anger, I called it. But it was anger that had gone underground and mixed itself with all kinds of other emotions. To judge from its odd effects, it was anger disguised and complex, not anger simple and open.

Whatever the reason, all these books, I thought, surveying the pile on the desk, are worthless for my purposes. They were worthless scientifically, that is to say, though humanly they were full of instruction, interest, boredom, and very queer facts about the habits of the Fiji Islanders. They had been written in the red light of emotion and not in the white light of truth. Therefore they must be returned to the central desk and restored each to his own cell in the enormous honeycomb. All that I had retrieved from that morning's work had been the one fact of anger. The professors—I lumped them together thus—were angry. But why, I asked myself, having returned the books, why, I repeated, standing under the colonnade among the pigeons and the prehistoric canoes, why are they angry? And, asking myself this question, I strolled off to find a place for luncheon. What is the real nature of what I call for the moment their anger? I asked. Here was a puzzle that would last all the time that it takes to be served with food in a small restaurant somewhere near the British Museum. Some previous luncher had left the lunch edition of the evening paper on a chair, and, waiting to be served, I began idly reading the headlines. A ribbon of very large letters ran across the page. Somebody had made a big score in South Africa. Lesser ribbons announced that Sir Austen Chamberlain was at Geneva. A meat axe with human hair on it had been found in a cellar. Mr. Justice —— commented in the Divorce Courts upon the Shamelessness of Women. Sprinkled about the paper were other pieces of news. A film actress had been lowered from a peak in California and hung suspended in mid-air. The weather was going to be foggy. The most transient visitor to this planet, I thought, who picked up this paper could not fail to be aware, even from this scattered testimony, that England is under the rule of a patriarchy. Nobody in their senses could fail to detect the dominance of the professor. His was the power and the money and the influence. He was the proprietor of the paper and its editor and subeditor. He was the Foreign Secretary and the Judge. He was the cricketer; he owned the racehorses and the yachts. He was the director of the company that pays two hundred per cent to its shareholders. He left millions to charities and colleges that were ruled by himself. He suspended the film actress in mid-air. He will decide if the hair on the meat axe is human; he it is who will acquit or convict the murderer, and hang him, or let him go free. With the exception of the fog he seemed to control everything. Yet he was angry. I knew that he was angry by this token. When I read what he wrote about women I thought, not of what he was saying, but of himself. When an arguer argues dispassionately he thinks only of the argument; and the reader cannot help thinking of the argument too. If he had written dispassionately about women, had used indisputable proofs to establish his argument and had shown no trace of wishing that the result should be one thing rather than another, one would not have been angry either. One would have accepted the fact, as one accepts the fact that a pea is green or a canary yellow. So be it, I should have said. But I had been angry because he was angry. Yet it seemed absurd, I thought, turning over the evening paper, that a man with all this power should be angry. Or is anger, I wondered, somehow, the familiar, the attendant sprite on power? Rich people, for example, are often angry because they suspect that the poor want to seize their wealth. The professors, or patriarchs, as it might be more accurate to call them, might be angry for that reason partly, but partly for one that lies a little less obviously on the surface. Possibly they were not "angry" at all; often, indeed, they were admiring, devoted, exemplary in the relations of private life. Possibly when the professor insisted a little too emphatically upon the inferiority of women, he was concerned not with their inferiority, but with his own superiority. That was what he was protecting rather hot-headedly and with too much emphasis, because it was a jewel to him of the rarest price. Life for both sexes—and I looked at them, shouldering their way along the pavement—is arduous, difficult, a perpetual struggle. It calls for gigantic courage and strength. More than anything, perhaps, creatures of illusion as we are, it calls for confidence in oneself. Without self-confidence we are as babes in the cradle. And how can we generate this imponderable quality, which is yet so invaluable, most quickly? By thinking that other people are inferior to oneself. By feeling that one has some innate superiority—it may be wealth, or rank, a straight nose, or the portrait of a grandfather by Romney—for there is no end to the pathetic devices of the human imagination—over other people. Hence the enormous importance to a patriarch who has to conquer, who has to rule, of feeling that great numbers of people, half the human race indeed, are by nature inferior to himself. It must indeed be one of the chief sources of his power. But let me turn the light of this observation on to real life, I thought. Does it help to explain some of those psychological puzzles that one notes in the margin of daily life? Does it explain my astonishment of the other day when Z, most humane, most modest of men, taking up some book by Rebecca West and reading a passage in it, exclaimed, "The arrant feminist! She says that men are snobs!" The exclamation, to me so surprising—for why was Miss West an arrant feminist for making a possibly true if uncomplimentary statement about the other sex?—was not merely the cry of wounded vanity; it was a protest against some infringement of his power to believe in himself. Women have served all these centuries as looking-glasses possessing the magic and delicious power of reflecting the figure of man at twice its natural size. Without that power probably the earth would still be swamp and jungle. The glories of all our wars would be unknown. We should still be scratching the outlines of deer on the remains of mutton bones and bartering flints for sheepskins or whatever simple ornament took our unsophisticated taste. Supermen and Fingers of Destiny would never have existed. The Czar and the Kaiser would never have worn crowns or lost them. Whatever may be their use in civilised societies, mirrors are essential to all violent and heroic action. That is why Napoleon and Mussolini both insist

so emphatically upon the inferiority of women, for if they were
not inferior, they would cease to enlarge. That serves to explain
in part the necessity that women so often are to men. And it
serves to explain how restless they are under her criticism; how
impossible it is for her to say to them this book is bad, this picture is feeble, or whatever it may be, without giving far more
pain and rousing far more anger than a man would do who gave
the same criticism. For if she begins to tell the truth, the figure
in the looking-glass shrinks; his fitness for life is diminished.
How is he to go on giving judgement, civilising natives, making
laws, writing books, dressing up and speechifying at banquets,
unless he can see himself at breakfast and at dinner at least twice
the size he really is? So I reflected, crumbling my bread and stirring my coffee and now and again looking at the people in the
street. The looking-glass vision is of supreme importance because it charges the vitality; it stimulates the nervous system.
Take it away and man may die, like the drug fiend deprived of
his cocaine. Under the spell of that illusion, I thought, looking
out of the window, half the people on the pavement are striding
to work. They put on their hats and coats in the morning under
its agreeable rays. They start the day confident, braced, believ-
ing themselves desired at Miss Smith's tea party; they say to
themselves as they go into the room, I am the superior of half
the people here, and it is thus that they speak with that self-
confidence, that self-assurance, which have had such profound
consequences in public life and lead to such curious notes in the
margin of the private mind.

But these contributions to the dangerous and fascinating
subject of the psychology of the other sex—it is one, I hope,
that you will investigate when you have five hundred a year of
your own—were interrupted by the necessity of paying the bill.
It came to five shillings and ninepence. I gave the waiter a ten-
shilling note and he went to bring me change. There was an-

other ten-shilling note in my purse; I noticed it, because it is a fact that still takes my breath away—the power of my purse to breed ten-shilling notes automatically. I open it and there they are. Society gives me chicken and coffee, bed and lodging, in return for a certain number of pieces of paper which were left me by an aunt, for no other reason than that I share her name.

My aunt, Mary Beton, I must tell you, died by a fall from her horse when she was riding out to take the air in Bombay. The news of my legacy reached me one night about the same time that the act was passed that gave votes to women. A solicitor's letter fell into the post-box and when I opened it I found that she had left me five hundred pounds a year for ever. Of the two—the vote and the money—the money, I own, seemed infinitely the more important. Before that I had made my living by cadging odd jobs from newspapers, by reporting a donkey show here or a wedding there; I had earned a few pounds by addressing envelopes, reading to old ladies, making artificial flowers, teaching the alphabet to small children in a kindergarten. Such were the chief occupations that were open to women before 1918. I need not, I am afraid, describe in any detail the hardness of the work, for you know perhaps women who have done it; nor the difficulty of living on the money when it was earned, for you may have tried. But what still remains with me as a worse infliction than either was the poison of fear and bitterness which those days bred in me. To begin with, always to be doing work that one did not wish to do, and to do it like a slave, flattering and fawning, not always necessarily perhaps, but it seemed necessary and the stakes were too great to run risks; and then the thought of that one gift which it was death to hide—a small one but dear to the possessor—perishing and with it myself, my soul—all this became like a rust eating away the bloom of the spring, destroying the tree at its heart. However, as I say, my aunt died; and whenever I change a ten-shilling

note a little of that rust and corrosion is rubbed off; fear and
bitterness go. Indeed, I thought, slipping the silver into my
purse, it is remarkable, remembering the bitterness of those
days, what a change of temper a fixed income will bring about.
No force in the world can take from me my five hundred
pounds. Food, house and clothing are mine for ever. Therefore
not merely do effort and labour cease, but also hatred and bitterness. I need not hate any man; he cannot hurt me. I need not
flatter any man; he has nothing to give me. So imperceptibly I
found myself adopting a new attitude towards the other half of
the human race. It was absurd to blame any class or any sex, as
a whole. Great bodies of people are never responsible for what
they do. They are driven by instincts which are not within their
control. They too, the patriarchs, the professors, had endless
difficulties, terrible drawbacks to contend with. Their education
had been in some ways as faulty as my own. It had bred in them
defects as great. True, they had money and power, but only at
the cost of harbouring in their breasts an eagle, a vulture, for
ever tearing the liver out and plucking at the lungs—the instinct
for possession, the rage for acquisition which drives them to desire other people's fields and goods perpetually; to make fron-
tiers and flags; battleships and poison gas; to offer up their own
lives and their children's lives. Walk through the Admiralty Arch
(I had reached that monument), or any other avenue given up
to trophies and cannon, and reflect upon the kind of glory celebrated there. Or watch in the spring sunshine the stockbroker
and the great barrister going indoors to make money and more
money and more money when it is a fact that five hundred
pounds a year will keep one alive in the sunshine. These are unpleasant instincts to harbour, I reflected. They are bred of the
conditions of life; of the lack of civilisation, I thought, looking
at the statue of the Duke of Cambridge, and in particular at the
feathers in his cocked hat, with a fixity that they have scarcely

ever received before. And, as I realised these drawbacks, by degrees fear and bitterness modified themselves into pity and toleration; and then in a year or two, pity and toleration went, and
the greatest release of all came, which is freedom to think of
things in themselves. That building, for example, do I like it or
not? Is that picture beautiful or not? Is that in my opinion a
good book or a bad? Indeed my aunt's legacy unveiled the sky
to me, and substituted for the large and imposing figure of a
gentleman, which Milton recommended for my perpetual ado-
ration, a view of the open sky.

So thinking, so speculating, I found my way back to my
house by the river. Lamps were being lit and an indescribable
change had come over London since the morning hour. It was
as if the great machine after labouring all day had made with our
help a few yards of something very exciting and beautiful—a
fiery fabric flashing with red eyes, a tawny monster roaring with
hot breath. Even the wind seemed flung like a flag as it lashed
the houses and rattled the hoardings.

In my little street, however, domesticity prevailed. The
house painter was descending his ladder; the nursemaid was
wheeling the perambulator carefully in and out back to nursery
tea; the coal-heaver was folding his empty sacks on top of
each other; the woman who keeps the green-grocer's shop was
adding up the day's takings with her hands in red mittens. But
so engrossed was I with the problem you have laid upon my
shoulders that I could not see even these usual sights without
referring them to one centre. I thought how much harder it is
now than it must have been even a century ago to say which of
these employments is the higher, the more necessary. Is it better to be a coal-heaver or a nursemaid; is the charwoman who
has brought up eight children of less value to the world than the
barrister who has made a hundred thousand pounds? It is useless to ask such questions; for nobody can answer them. Not

only do the comparative values of charwomen and lawyers rise and fall from decade to decade, but we have no rods with which to measure them even as they are at the moment. I had been foolish to ask my professor to furnish me with "indisputable proofs" of this or that in his argument about women. Even if one could state the value of any one gift at the moment, those values will change; in a century's time very possibly they will have changed completely. Moreover, in a hundred years, I thought, reaching my own doorstep, women will have ceased to be the protected sex. Logically they will take part in all the activities and exertions that were once denied them. The nursemaid will heave coal. The shop-woman will drive an engine. All assumptions founded on the facts observed when women were the protected sex will have disappeared—as, for example (here a squad of soldiers marched down the street), that women and clergymen and gardeners live longer than other people. Remove that protection, expose them to the same exertions and activities, make them soldiers and sailors and engine-drivers and dock labourers, and will not women die off so much younger, so much quicker, than men that one will say, "I saw a woman today," as one used to say, "I saw an aeroplane." Anything may happen when womanhood has ceased to be a protected occupation, I thought, opening the door. But what bearing has all this upon the subject of my paper, Women and Fiction? I asked, going indoors.

CHAPTER THREE

IT WAS disappointing not to have brought back in the evening some important statement, some authentic fact. Women are poorer than men because—this or that. Perhaps now it would be better to give up seeking for the truth, and receiving on one's head an avalanche of opinion hot as lava, discoloured as dishwater. It would be better to draw the curtains; to shut out distractions; to light the lamp; to narrow the enquiry and to ask the historian, who records not opinions but facts, to describe under what conditions women lived, not throughout the ages, but in England, say in the time of Elizabeth.

For it is a perennial puzzle why no woman wrote a word of that extraordinary literature when every other man, it seemed, was capable of song or sonnet. What were the conditions in which women lived, I asked myself; for fiction, imaginative work that is, is not dropped like a pebble upon the ground, as science may be; fiction is like a spider's web, attached ever so lightly perhaps, but still attached to life at all four corners. Often the attachment is scarcely perceptible; Shakespeare's plays, for instance, seem to hang there complete by themselves. But when the web is pulled askew, hooked up at the edge, torn in the middle, one remembers that these webs are not spun in mid-air by incorporeal creatures, but are the work of suffering human beings, and are attached to grossly material things, like health and money and the houses we live in.

I went, therefore, to the shelf where the histories stand and took down one of the latest, Professor Trevelyan's *History of England*. Once more I looked up Women, found "position of," and turned to the pages indicated. "Wife-beating," I read, "was a recognised right of man, and was practised without shame by high as well as low. . . . Similarly," the historian goes on, "the daughter who refused to marry the gentleman of her parents' choice was liable to be locked up, beaten and flung about the room, without any shock being inflicted on public opinion. Marriage was not an affair of personal affection, but of family avarice, particularly in the 'chivalrous' upper classes. . . . Betrothal often took place while one or both of the parties was in the cradle, and marriage when they were scarcely out of the nurses' charge." That was about 1470, soon after Chaucer's time. The next reference to the position of women is some two hundred years later, in the time of the Stuarts. "It was still the exception for women of the upper and middle class to choose their own husbands, and when the husband had been assigned, he was lord and master, so far at least as law and custom could make him. Yet even so," Professor Trevelyan concludes, "neither Shakespeare's women nor those of authentic seventeenth-century memoirs, like the Verneys and the Hutchinsons, seem wanting in personality and character." Certainly, if we consider it, Cleopatra must have had a way with her; Lady Macbeth, one would suppose, had a will of her own; Rosalind, one might conclude, was an attractive girl. Professor Trevelyan is speaking no more than the truth when he remarks that Shakespeare's women do not seem wanting in personality and character. Not being a historian, one might go even further and say that women have burnt like beacons in all the works of all the poets from the beginning of time—Clytemnestra, Antigone, Cleopatra, Lady Macbeth, Phèdre, Cressida, Rosalind, Desdemona, the Duchess of Malfi, among the dramatists; then among the prose writers: Millamant, Clarissa, Becky Sharp, Anna Karenina, Emma Bovary, Madame de Guermantes—the names flock to mind, nor do they recall women "lacking in personality and character." Indeed, if woman had no existence save in the fiction written by men, one would imagine her a person of the utmost importance; very various; heroic and mean; splendid and sordid; infinitely beautiful and hideous in the extreme; as great as a man, some think even greater.[1] But this is woman in fiction. In fact, as Professor Trevelyan points out, she was locked up, beaten and flung about the room.

A very queer, composite being thus emerges. Imaginatively she is of the highest importance; practically she is completely insignificant. She pervades poetry from cover to cover; she is all but absent from history. She dominates the lives of kings and conquerors in fiction; in fact she was the slave of any boy whose parents forced a ring upon her finger. Some of the most inspired words, some of the most profound thoughts in literature fall from her lips; in real life she could hardly read, could scarcely spell, and was the property of her husband.

---

[1]"It remains a strange and almost inexplicable fact that in Athena's city, where women were kept in almost Oriental suppression as odalisques or drudges, the stage should yet have produced figures like Clytemnestra and Cassandra, Atossa and Antigone, Phèdre and Medea, and all the other heroines who dominate play after play of the 'misogynist' Euripides. But the paradox of this world where in real life a respectable woman could hardly show her face alone in the street, and yet on the stage woman equals or surpasses man, has never been satisfactorily explained. In modern tragedy the same predominance exists. At all events, a very cursory survey of Shakespeare's work (similarly with Webster, though not with Marlowe or Jonson) suffices to reveal how this dominance, this initiative of women, persists from Rosalind to Lady Macbeth. So too in Racine; six of his tragedies bear their heroines' names; and what male characters of his shall we set against Hermione and Andromaque, Bérénice and Roxane, Phèdre and Athalie? So again with Ibsen; what men shall we match with Solveig and Nora, Hedda and Hilda Wangel and Rebecca West?"—F. L. LUCAS, *Tragedy*, pp. 114–15.

It was certainly an odd monster that one made up by reading the historians first and the poets afterwards—a worm winged
like an eagle; the spirit of life and beauty in a kitchen chopping
up suet. But these monsters, however amusing to the imagination, have no existence in fact. What one must do to bring her
to life was to think poetically and prosaically at one and the
same moment, thus keeping in touch with fact—that she is
Mrs. Martin, aged thirty-six, dressed in blue, wearing a black hat
and brown shoes; but not losing sight of fiction either—that
she is a vessel in which all sorts of spirits and forces are cours-
ing and flashing perpetually. The moment, however, that one
tries this method with the Elizabethan woman, one branch of
illumination fails; one is held up by the scarcity of facts. One
knows nothing detailed, nothing perfectly true and substantial
about her. History scarcely mentions her. And I turned to Professor Trevelyan again to see what history meant to him. I
found by looking at his chapter headings that it meant—

"The Manor Court and the Methods of Open-field Agricul-
ture . . . The Cistercians and Sheep-farming . . . The Crusades . . .
The University . . . The House of Commons . . . The Hundred
Years' War . . . The Wars of the Roses . . . The Renaissance
Scholars . . . The Dissolution of the Monasteries . . . Agrarian
and Religious Strife . . . The Origin of English Sea-power . . .
The Armada . . ." and so on. Occasionally an individual woman
is mentioned, an Elizabeth, or a Mary; a queen or a great lady.
But by no possible means could middle-class women with nothing but brains and character at their command have taken part
in any one of the great movements which, brought together,
constitute the historian's view of the past. Nor shall we find her
in any collection of anecdotes. Aubrey hardly mentions her. She
never writes her own life and scarcely keeps a diary; there are
only a handful of her letters in existence. She left no plays
or poems by which we can judge her. What one wants, I

thought—and why does not some brilliant student at Newnham or Girton supply it?—is a mass of information; at what
age did she marry; how many children had she as a rule; what
was her house like; had she a room to herself; did she do the
cooking; would she be likely to have a servant? All these facts
lie somewhere, presumably, in parish registers and account
books; the life of the average Elizabethan woman must be scattered about somewhere, could one collect it and make a book
of it. It would be ambitious beyond my daring, I thought, looking about the shelves for books that were not there, to suggest
to the students of those famous colleges that they should re-
write history, though I own that it often seems a little queer as
it is, unreal, lop-sided; but why should they not add a supplement to history? calling it, of course, by some inconspicuous
name so that women might figure there without impropriety?
For one often catches a glimpse of them in the lives of the great,
whisking away into the background, concealing, I sometimes
think, a wink, a laugh, perhaps a tear. And, after all, we have lives
enough of Jane Austen; it scarcely seems necessary to consider
again the influence of the tragedies of Joanna Baillie upon the
poetry of Edgar Allan Poe; as for myself, I should not mind if
the homes and haunts of Mary Russell Mitford were closed to
the public for a century at least. But what I find deplorable, I
continued, looking about the bookshelves again, is that nothing
is known about women before the eighteenth century. I have no
model in my mind to turn about this way and that. Here am I
asking why women did not write poetry in the Elizabethan age,
and I am not sure how they were educated; whether they were
taught to write; whether they had sitting-rooms to themselves;
how many women had children before they were twenty-one;
what, in short, they did from eight in the morning till eight at
night. They had no money evidently; according to Professor
Trevelyan they were married whether they liked it or not before

they were out of the nursery, at fifteen or sixteen very likely. It would have been extremely odd, even upon this showing, had one of them suddenly written the plays of Shakespeare, I concluded, and I thought of that old gentleman, who is dead now, but was a bishop, I think, who declared that it was impossible for any woman, past, present, or to come, to have the genius of Shakespeare. He wrote to the papers about it. He also told a lady who applied to him for information that cats do not as a matter of fact go to heaven, though they have, he added, souls of a sort. How much thinking those old gentlemen used to save one! How the borders of ignorance shrank back at their approach! Cats do not go to heaven. Women cannot write the plays of Shakespeare.

Be that as it may, I could not help thinking, as I looked at the works of Shakespeare on the shelf, that the bishop was right at least in this; it would have been impossible, completely and entirely, for any woman to have written the plays of Shakespeare in the age of Shakespeare. Let me imagine, since facts are so hard to come by, what would have happened had Shakespeare had a wonderfully gifted sister, called Judith, let us say. Shakespeare himself went, very probably—his mother was an heiress—to the grammar school, where he may have learnt Latin—Ovid, Virgil and Horace—and the elements of grammar and logic. He was, it is well known, a wild boy who poached rabbits, perhaps shot a deer, and had, rather sooner than he should have done, to marry a woman in the neighbourhood, who bore him a child rather quicker than was right. That escapade sent him to seek his fortune in London. He had, it seemed, a taste for the theatre; he began by holding horses at the stage door. Very soon he got work in the theatre, became a successful actor, and lived at the hub of the universe, meeting everybody, knowing everybody, practising his art on the boards, exercising his wits in the streets, and even getting access to the palace of the queen. Meanwhile his extraordinarily gifted sister, let us suppose, remained at home. She was as adventurous, as imaginative, as agog to see the world as he was. But she was not sent to school. She had no chance of learning grammar and logic, let alone of reading Horace and Virgil. She picked up a book now and then, one of her brother's perhaps, and read a few pages. But then her parents came in and told her to mend the stockings or mind the stew and not moon about with books and papers. They would have spoken sharply but kindly, for they were substantial people who knew the conditions of life for a woman and loved their daughter—indeed, more likely than not she was the apple of her father's eye. Perhaps she scribbled some pages up in an apple loft on the sly, but was careful to hide them or set fire to them. Soon, however, before she was out of her teens, she was to be betrothed to the son of a neighbouring wool-stapler. She cried out that marriage was hateful to her, and for that she was severely beaten by her father. Then he ceased to scold her. He begged her instead not to hurt him, not to shame him in this matter of her marriage. He would give her a chain of beads or a fine petticoat, he said; and there were tears in his eyes. How could she disobey him? How could she break his heart? The force of her own gift alone drove her to it. She made up a small parcel of her belongings, let herself down by a rope one summer's night and took the road to London. She was not seventeen. The birds that sang in the hedge were not more musical than she was. She had the quickest fancy, a gift like her brother's, for the tune of words. Like him, she had a taste for the theatre. She stood at the stage door; she wanted to act, she said. Men laughed in her face. The manager—a fat, loose-lipped man—guffawed. He bellowed something about poodles danc-ing and women acting—no woman, he said, could possibly be an actress. He hinted—you can imagine what. She could get no training in her craft. Could she even seek her dinner in a tavern or roam the streets at midnight? Yet her genius was for fiction and lusted to feed abundantly upon the lives of men and women and the study of their ways. At last—for she was very young, oddly like Shakespeare the poet in her face, with the same grey eyes and rounded brows—at last Nick Greene the actor-manager took pity on her; she found herself with child by that gentleman and so—who shall measure the heat and violence of the poet's heart when caught and tangled in a woman's body?—killed herself one winter's night and lies buried at some cross-roads where the omnibuses now stop outside the Elephant and Castle.

That, more or less, is how the story would run, I think, if a woman in Shakespeare's day had had Shakespeare's genius. But for my part, I agree with the deceased bishop, if such he was—it is unthinkable that any woman in Shakespeare's day should have had Shakespeare's genius. For genius like Shakespeare's is not born among labouring, uneducated, servile people. It was not born in England among the Saxons and the Britons. It is not born today among the working classes. How, then, could it have been born among women whose work began, according to Professor Trevelyan, almost before they were out of the nursery, who were forced to it by their parents and held to it by all the power of law and custom? Yet genius of a sort must have existed among women as it must have existed among the working classes. Now and again an Emily Brontë or a Robert Burns blazes out and proves its presence. But certainly it never got itself on to paper. When, however, one reads of a witch being ducked, of a woman possessed by devils, of a wise woman selling herbs, or even of a very remarkable man who had a mother, then I think we are on the track of a lost novelist, a suppressed poet, of some mute and inglorious Jane Austen, some Emily Brontë who dashed her brains out on the moor or mopped and mowed about the highways crazed with the torture that her gift had put her to. Indeed, I would venture to guess that Anon, who wrote so many poems without signing them, was often a woman. It was a woman Edward Fitzgerald, I think, suggested who made the ballads and the folk-songs, crooning them to her children, beguiling her spinning with them, or the length of the winter's night.

This may be true or it may be false—who can say?—but what is true in it, so it seemed to me, reviewing the story of Shakespeare's sister as I had made it, is that any woman born with a great gift in the sixteenth century would certainly have gone crazed, shot herself, or ended her days in some lonely cottage outside the village, half witch, half wizard, feared and mocked at. For it needs little skill in psychology to be sure that a highly gifted girl who had tried to use her gift for poetry would have been so thwarted and hindered by other people, so tortured and pulled asunder by her own contrary instincts, that she must have lost her health and sanity to a certainty. No girl could have walked to London and stood at a stage door and forced her way into the presence of actor-managers without doing herself a violence and suffering an anguish which may have been irrational—for chastity may be a fetish invented by certain societies for unknown reasons—but were none the less inevitable. Chastity had then, it has even now, a religious importance in a woman's life, and has so wrapped itself round with nerves and instincts that to cut it free and bring it to the light of day demands courage of the rarest. To have lived a free life in London in the sixteenth century would have meant for a woman who was poet and playwright a nervous stress and dilemma which might well have killed her. Had she survived, whatever she had written would have been twisted and deformed, issuing from a strained and morbid imagination. And undoubtedly, I thought, looking at the shelf where there are no plays by women, her work would have gone unsigned. That refuge she would have sought certainly. It was the relic of the sense of chastity that dictated anonymity to women even so late as the nineteenth century. Currer Bell, George Eliot, George Sand, all the victims of inner strife as their writings prove, sought ineffectively to veil themselves by using the name of a man. Thus they did homage to the convention, which if not implanted by the other sex was liberally encouraged by them (the chief glory of a woman is not to be talked of, said Pericles, himself a much-talked-of man), that publicity in women is detestable. Anonymity runs in their blood. The desire to be veiled still possesses them. They are not even now as concerned about the health of their fame as men are, and, speaking generally, will pass a tombstone or a signpost without feeling an irresistible desire to cut their names on it, as Alf, Bert or Chas. must do in obedience to their instinct, which murmurs if it sees a fine woman go by, or even a dog, *Ce chien est à moi.* And, of course, it may not be a dog, I thought, remembering Parliament Square, the Sièges Allée and other avenues; it may be a piece of land or a man with curly black hair. It is one of the great advantages of being a woman that one can pass even a very fine negress without wishing to make an Englishwoman of her.

That woman, then, who was born with a gift of poetry in the sixteenth century, was an unhappy woman, a woman at strife against herself. All the conditions of her life, all her own instincts, were hostile to the state of mind which is needed to set free whatever is in the brain. But what is the state of mind that is most propitious to the act of creation, I asked. Can one come by any notion of the state that furthers and makes possible that strange activity? Here I opened the volume containing the Tragedies of Shakespeare. What was Shakespeare's state of mind, for instance, when he wrote *Lear* and *Antony and Cleopatra?* It was certainly the state of mind most favourable to poetry that there has ever existed. But Shakespeare himself said nothing about it. We only know casually and by chance that he "never blotted a line." Nothing indeed was ever said by the artist himself about his state of mind until the eighteenth century perhaps. Rousseau perhaps began it. At any rate, by the nineteenth century self-consciousness had developed so far that it was the habit for men of letters to describe their minds in confessions and autobiographies. Their lives also were written, and their letters were printed after their deaths. Thus, though we do not know what Shakespeare went through when he wrote *Lear,* we do know what Carlyle went through when he wrote the *French Revolution*; what Flaubert went through when he wrote *Madame Bovary*; what Keats was going through when he tried to write poetry against the coming of death and the indifference of the world.

And one gathers from this enormous modern literature of confession and self-analysis that to write a work of genius is almost always a feat of prodigious difficulty. Everything is against the likelihood that it will come from the writer's mind whole and entire. Generally material circumstances are against it. Dogs will bark; people will interrupt; money must be made; health will break down. Further, accentuating all these difficulties and making them harder to bear is the world's notorious indifference. It does not ask people to write poems and novels and histories; it does not need them. It does not care whether Flaubert finds the right word or whether Carlyle scrupulously verifies this or that fact. Naturally, it will not pay for what it does not want. And so the writer, Keats, Flaubert, Carlyle, suffers, especially in the creative years of youth, every form of distraction and discouragement. A curse, a cry of agony, rises from those books of analysis and confession. "Mighty poets in their misery dead"—that is the burden of their song. If anything comes through in spite of all this, it is a miracle, and probably no book is born entire and uncrippled as it was conceived.

But for women, I thought, looking at the empty shelves, these difficulties were infinitely more formidable. In the first place, to have a room of her own, let alone a quiet room or a sound-proof room, was out of the question, unless her parents were exceptionally rich or very noble, even up to the beginning of the nineteenth century. Since her pin money, which depended on the good will of her father, was only enough to keep her clothed, she was debarred from such alleviations as came even to Keats or Tennyson or Carlyle, all poor men, from a walking tour, a little journey to France, from the separate lodging which, even if it were miserable enough, sheltered them from the claims and tyrannies of their families. Such material difficulties were formidable; but much worse were the immaterial. The indifference of the world which Keats and Flaubert and other men of genius have found so hard to bear was in her case not indifference but hostility. The world did not say to her as it said to them, Write if you choose; it makes no difference to me. The world said with a guffaw, Write? What's the good of your writing? Here the psychologists of Newnham and Girton might come to our help, I thought, looking again at the blank spaces on the shelves. For surely it is time that the effect of discouragement upon the mind of the artist should be measured, as I have seen a dairy company measure the effect of ordinary milk and Grade A milk upon the body of the rat. They set two rats in cages side by side, and of the two one was furtive, timid and small, and the other was glossy, bold and big. Now what food do we feed women as artists upon? I asked, remembering, I suppose, that dinner of prunes and custard. To answer that question I had only to open the evening paper and to read that Lord Birkenhead is of opinion—but really I am not going to trouble to copy out Lord Birkenhead's opinion upon the writing of women. What Dean Inge says I will leave in peace. The Harley Street specialist may be allowed to rouse the echoes of

Harley Street with his vociferations without raising a hair on my head. I will quote, however, Mr. Oscar Browning, because Mr. Oscar Browning was a great figure in Cambridge at one time, and used to examine the students at Girton and Newnham. Mr. Oscar Browning was wont to declare "that the impression left on his mind, after looking over any set of examination papers, was that, irrespective of the marks he might give, the best woman was intellectually the inferior of the worst man." After saying that Mr. Browning went back to his rooms—and it is this sequel that endears him and makes him a human figure of some bulk and majesty—he went back to his rooms and found a stable-boy lying on the sofa—"a mere skeleton, his cheeks were cavernous and sallow, his teeth were black, and he did not appear to have the full use of his limbs. . . . 'That's Arthur' [said Mr. Browning]. 'He's a dear boy really and most high-minded.'" The two pictures always seem to me to complete each other. And happily in this age of biography the two pictures often do complete each other, so that we are able to interpret the opinions of great men not only by what they say, but by what they do.

But though this is possible now, such opinions coming from the lips of important people must have been formidable enough even fifty years ago. Let us suppose that a father from the highest motives did not wish his daughter to leave home and become writer, painter or scholar. "See what Mr. Oscar Browning says," he would say; and there was not only Mr. Oscar Browning; there was the *Saturday Review*; there was Mr. Greg—the "essentials of a woman's being," said Mr. Greg emphatically, "are that *they are supported by, and they minister to, men*"—there was an enormous body of masculine opinion to the effect that nothing could be expected of women intellectually. Even if her father did not read out loud these opinions, any girl could read them for herself; and the reading, even in the nineteenth century, must have lowered her vitality, and told profoundly upon her

work. There would always have been that assertion—you cannot do this, you are incapable of doing that—to protest against,
to overcome. Probably for a novelist this germ is no longer of
much effect; for there have been women novelists of merit. But
for painters it must still have some sting in it; and for musicians,
I imagine, is even now active and poisonous in the extreme. The
woman composer stands where the actress stood in the time of
Shakespeare. Nick Greene, I thought, remembering the story I
had made about Shakespeare's sister, said that a woman acting
put him in mind of a dog dancing. Johnson repeated the phrase
two hundred years later of women preaching. And here, I said,
opening a book about music, we have the very words used again
in this year of grace, 1928, of women who try to write music.
"Of Mlle. Germaine Tailleferre one can only repeat Dr. Johnson's dictum concerning a woman preacher, transposed into
terms of music. 'Sir, a woman's composing is like a dog's walking on his hind legs. It is not done well, but you are surprised to
find it done at all.'"[2] So accurately does history repeat itself.

Thus, I concluded, shutting Mr. Oscar Browning's life and
pushing away the rest, it is fairly evident that even in the nineteenth century a woman was not encouraged to be an artist. On
the contrary, she was snubbed, slapped, lectured and exhorted.
Her mind must have been strained and her vitality lowered by
the need of opposing this, of disproving that. For here again we
come within range of that very interesting and obscure masculine complex which has had so much influence upon the
woman's movement; that deep-seated desire, not so much that
she shall be inferior as that *he* shall be superior, which plants him
wherever one looks, not only in front of the arts, but barring the
way to politics too, even when the risk to himself seems infini-
tesimal and the suppliant humble and devoted. Even Lady Bess-

[2]*A Survey of Contemporary Music,* Cecil Gray, p. 246.

borough, I remembered, with all her passion for politics, must humbly bow herself and write to Lord Granville Leveson-Gower: "...notwithstanding all my violence in politics and talking so much on that subject, I perfectly agree with you that no woman has any business to meddle with that or any other serious business, farther than giving her opinion (if she is ask'd)." And so she goes on to spend her enthusiasm where it meets with no obstacle whatsoever upon that immensely important subject, Lord Granville's maiden speech in the House of Commons. The spectacle is certainly a strange one, I thought. The history of men's opposition to women's emancipation is more interesting perhaps than the story of that emancipation itself. An amusing book might be made of it if some young student at Girton or Newnham would collect examples and deduce a theory—but she would need thick gloves on her hands, and bars to protect her of solid gold.

But what is amusing now, I recollected, shutting Lady Bessborough, had to be taken in desperate earnest once. Opinions that one now pastes in a book labelled cock-a-doodle-dum and keeps for reading to select audiences on summer nights once drew tears, I can assure you. Among your grandmothers and great-grandmothers there were many that wept their eyes out. Florence Nightingale shrieked aloud in her agony.[3] Moreover, it is all very well for you, who have got yourselves to college and enjoy sitting-rooms—or is it only bed-sitting-rooms?—of your own to say that genius should disregard such opinions; that genius should be above caring what is said of it. Unfortunately, it is precisely the men or women of genius who mind most what is said of them. Remember Keats. Remember the words he had cut on his tombstone. Think of Tennyson; think—but I need hardly multiply instances of the undeniable, if very unfortunate,

[3]See *Cassandra*, by Florence Nightingale, printed in *The Cause*, by R. Strachey.

fact that it is the nature of the artist to mind excessively what is said about him. Literature is strewn with the wreckage of men who have minded beyond reason the opinions of others.

And this susceptibility of theirs is doubly unfortunate, I thought, returning again to my original enquiry into what state of mind is most propitious for creative work, because the mind of an artist, in order to achieve the prodigious effort of freeing whole and entire the work that is in him, must be incandescent, like Shakespeare's mind, I conjectured, looking at the book which lay open at *Antony and Cleopatra*. There must be no obstacle in it, no foreign matter unconsumed.

For though we say that we know nothing about Shakespeare's state of mind, even as we say that, we are saying something about Shakespeare's state of mind. The reason perhaps why we know so little of Shakespeare—compared with Donne or Ben Jonson or Milton—is that his grudges and spites and antipathies are hidden from us. We are not held up by some "revelation" which reminds us of the writer. All desire to protest, to preach, to proclaim an injury, to pay off a score, to make the world the witness of some hardship or grievance was fired out of him and consumed. Therefore his poetry flows from him free and unimpeded. If ever a human being got his work expressed completely, it was Shakespeare. If ever a mind was incandescent, unimpeded, I thought, turning again to the bookcase, it was Shakespeare's mind.

CHAPTER FOUR

THAT ONE would find any woman in that state of mind in the sixteenth century was obviously impossible. One has only to think of the Elizabethan tombstones with all those children kneeling with clasped hands; and their early deaths; and to see their houses with their dark, cramped rooms, to realise that no woman could have written poetry then. What one would expect to find would be that rather later perhaps some great lady would take advantage of her comparative freedom and comfort to publish something with her name to it and risk being thought a monster. Men, of course, are not snobs, I continued, carefully eschewing "the arrant feminism" of Miss Rebecca West; but they appreciate with sympathy for the most part the efforts of a countess to write verse. One would expect to find a lady of title meeting with far greater encouragement than an unknown Miss Austen or a Miss Brontë at that time would have met with. But one would also expect to find that her mind was disturbed by alien emotions like fear and hatred and that her poems showed traces of that disturbance. Here is Lady Winchilsea, for example, I thought, taking down her poems. She was born in the year 1661; she was noble both by birth and by marriage; she was childless; she wrote poetry, and one has only to open her poetry to find her bursting out in indignation against the position of women:

> How are we fallen! fallen by mistaken rules,
> And Education's more than Nature's fools;
> Debarred from all improvements of the mind,
> And to be dull, expected and designed;
> And if some one would soar above the rest,
> With warmer fancy, and ambition pressed,
> So strong the opposing faction still appears,
> The hopes to thrive can ne'er outweigh the fears.

Clearly her mind has by no means "consumed all impediments and become incandescent." On the contrary, it is harassed and distracted with hates and grievances. The human race is split up for her into two parties. Men are the "opposing faction"; men are hated and feared, because they have the power to bar her way to what she wants to do—which is to write.

> Alas! a woman that attempts the pen,
> Such a presumptuous creature is esteemed,
> The fault can by no virtue be redeemed.
> They tell us we mistake our sex and way;
> Good breeding, fashion, dancing, dressing, play,
> Are the accomplishments we should desire;
> To write, or read, or think, or to enquire,
> Would cloud our beauty, and exhaust our time,
> And interrupt the conquests of our prime,
> Whilst the dull manage of a servile house
> Is held by some our utmost art and use.

Indeed she has to encourage herself to write by supposing that what she writes will never be published; to soothe herself with the sad chant:

To some few friends, and to thy sorrows sing,
For groves of laurel thou wert never meant;
Be dark enough thy shades, and be thou there content.

Yet it is clear that could she have freed her mind from hate and fear and not heaped it with bitterness and resentment, the fire was hot within her. Now and again words issue of pure poetry:

Nor will in fading silks compose,
Faintly the inimitable rose.

—they are rightly praised by Mr. Murry, and Pope, it is thought, remembered and appropriated those others:

Now the jonquille o'ercomes the feeble brain;
We faint beneath the aromatic pain.

It was a thousand pities that the woman who could write like that, whose mind was turned to nature and reflection, should have been forced to anger and bitterness. But how could she have helped herself? I asked, imagining the sneers and the laughter, the adulation of the toadies, the scepticism of the professional poet. She must have shut herself up in a room in the country to write, and been torn asunder by bitterness and scruples perhaps, though her husband was of the kindest, and their married life perfection. She "must have," I say, because when one comes to seek out the facts about Lady Winchilsea, one finds, as usual, that almost nothing is known about her. She suffered terribly from melancholy, which we can explain at least to some extent when we find her telling us how in the grip of it she would imagine:

My lines decried, and my employment thought
An useless folly or presumptuous fault:

The employment, which was thus censured, was, as far as one
can see, the harmless one of rambling about the fields and
dreaming:

My hand delights to trace unusual things,
And deviates from the known and common way,
Nor will in fading silks compose,
Faintly the inimitable rose.

Naturally, if that was her habit and that was her delight, she
could only expect to be laughed at; and, accordingly, Pope or
Gay is said to have satirised her "as a blue-stocking with an itch
for scribbling." Also it is thought that she offended Gay by
laughing at him. She said that his *Trivia* showed that "he was
more proper to walk before a chair than to ride in one." But this
is all "dubious gossip" and, says Mr. Murry, "uninteresting." But
there I do not agree with him, for I should have liked to have
had more even of dubious gossip so that I might have found
out or made up some image of this melancholy lady, who loved
wandering in the fields and thinking about unusual things and
scorned, so rashly, so unwisely, "the dull manage of a servile
house." But she became diffuse, Mr. Murry says. Her gift is all
grown about with weeds and bound with briars. It had no
chance of showing itself for the fine distinguished gift it was.
And so, putting her back on the shelf, I turned to the other great
lady, the Duchess whom Lamb loved, hare-brained, fantastical
Margaret of Newcastle, her elder, but her contemporary. They
were very different, but alike in this that both were noble and
both childless, and both were married to the best of husbands.
In both burnt the same passion for poetry and both are disfig-

ured and deformed by the same causes. Open the Duchess and one finds the same outburst of rage, "Women live like Bats or Owls, labour like Beasts, and die like Worms. . . ." Margaret too might have been a poet; in our day all that activity would have turned a wheel of some sort. As it was, what could bind, tame or civilise for human use that wild, generous, untutored intelligence? It poured itself out, higgledy-piggledy, in torrents of rhyme and prose, poetry and philosophy which stand congealed in quartos and folios that nobody ever reads. She should have had a microscope put in her hand. She should have been taught to look at the stars and reason scientifically. Her wits were turned with solitude and freedom. No one checked her. No one taught her. The professors fawned on her. At Court they jeered at her. Sir Egerton Brydges complained of her coarseness—"as flowing from a female of high rank brought up in the Courts." She shut herself up at Welbeck alone.

What a vision of loneliness and riot the thought of Margaret Cavendish brings to mind! as if some giant cucumber had spread itself over all the roses and carnations in the garden and choked them to death. What a waste that the woman who wrote "the best bred women are those whose minds are civilest" should have frittered her time away scribbling nonsense and plunging ever deeper into obscurity and folly till the people crowded round her coach when she issued out. Evidently the crazy Duchess became a bogey to frighten clever girls with. Here, I remembered, putting away the Duchess and opening Dorothy Osborne's letters, is Dorothy writing to Temple about the Duchess's new book. "Sure the poore woman is a little distracted, shee could never bee soe rediculous else as to venture at writeing book's and in verse too, if I should not sleep this fortnight I should not come to that."

And so, since no woman of sense and modesty could write books, Dorothy, who was sensitive and melancholy, the very opposite of the Duchess in temper, wrote nothing. Letters did not count. A woman might write letters while she was sitting by her father's sick-bed. She could write them by the fire whilst the men talked without disturbing them. The strange thing is, I thought, turning over the pages of Dorothy's letters, what a gift that untaught and solitary girl had for the framing of a sentence, for the fashioning of a scene. Listen to her running on:

"After dinner wee sitt and talk till Mr. B. com's in question and then I am gon. the heat of the day is spent in reading or working and about sixe or seven a Clock, I walke out into a Common that lyes hard by the house where a great many young wenches keep Sheep and Cow's and sitt in the shades singing of Ballads; I goe to them and compare their voyces and Beauty's to some Ancient Shepherdesses that I have read of and finde a vaste difference there, but trust mee I think these are as innocent as those could bee. I talke to them, and finde they want nothing to make them the happiest People in the world, but the knoledge that they are soe. most commonly when we are in the middest of our discourse one looks about her and spyes her Cow's goeing into the Corne and then away they all run, as if they had wing's at theire heels. I that am not soe nimble stay behinde, and when I see them driveing home theire Cattle I think tis time for mee to retyre too. when I have supped I goe into the Garden and soe to the syde of a small River that runs by it where I sitt downe and wish you with mee. . . ."

One could have sworn that she had the makings of a writer in her. But "if I should not sleep this fortnight I should not come to that"—one can measure the opposition that was in the air to a woman writing when one finds that even a woman with a great turn for writing has brought herself to believe that to write a book was to be ridiculous, even to show oneself distracted. And so we come, I continued, replacing the single short volume of Dorothy Osborne's letters upon the shelf, to Mrs. Behn.

And with Mrs. Behn we turn a very important corner on the road. We leave behind, shut up in their parks among their folios, those solitary great ladies who wrote without audience or criticism, for their own delight alone. We come to town and rub shoulders with ordinary people in the streets. Mrs. Behn was a middle-class woman with all the plebeian virtues of humour, vitality and courage; a woman forced by the death of her husband and some unfortunate adventures of her own to make her living by her wits. She had to work on equal terms with men. She made, by working very hard, enough to live on. The importance of that fact outweighs anything that she actually wrote, even the splendid "A Thousand Martyrs I have made," or "Love in Fantastic Triumph sat," for here begins the freedom of the mind, or rather the possibility that in the course of time the mind will be free to write what it likes. For now that Aphra Behn had done it, girls could go to their parents and say, You need not give me an allowance; I can make money by my pen. Of course the answer for many years to come was, Yes, by living the life of Aphra Behn! Death would be better! and the door was slammed faster than ever. That profoundly interesting subject, the value that men set upon women's chastity and its effect upon their education, here suggests itself for discussion, and might provide an interesting book if any student at Girton or Newnham cared to go into the matter. Lady Dudley, sitting in diamonds among the midges of a Scottish moor, might serve for frontispiece. Lord Dudley, *The Times* said when Lady Dudley died the other day, "a man of cultivated taste and many accomplishments, was benevolent and bountiful, but whimsically despotic. He insisted upon his wife's wearing full dress, even at the remotest shooting-lodge in the Highlands; he loaded her

with gorgeous jewels," and so on, "he gave her everything—
always excepting any measure of responsibility." Then Lord
Dudley had a stroke and she nursed him and ruled his estates
with supreme competence for ever after. That whimsical des-
potism was in the nineteenth century too.

But to return. Aphra Behn proved that money could be
made by writing at the sacrifice, perhaps, of certain agreeable
qualities; and so by degrees writing became not merely a sign of
folly and a distracted mind, but was of practical importance. A
husband might die, or some disaster overtake the family. Hundreds of women began as the eighteenth century drew on to add
to their pin money, or to come to the rescue of their families by
making translations or writing the innumerable bad novels
which have ceased to be recorded even in textbooks, but are to
be picked up in the fourpenny boxes in the Charing Cross Road.
The extreme activity of mind which showed itself in the later
eighteenth century among women—the talking, and the meeting, the writing of essays on Shakespeare, the translating of the
classics—was founded on the solid fact that women could
make money by writing. Money dignifies what is frivolous if un-
paid for. It might still be well to sneer at "blue stockings with
an itch for scribbling," but it could not be denied that they could
put money in their purses. Thus, towards the end of the eighteenth century a change came about which, if I were rewriting
history, I should describe more fully and think of greater importance than the Crusades or the Wars of the Roses. The middle-
class woman began to write. For if *Pride and Prejudice* matters,
and *Middlemarch* and *Villette* and *Wuthering Heights* matter, then
it matters far more than I can prove in an hour's discourse that
women generally, and not merely the lonely aristocrat shut up
in her country house among her folios and her flatterers, took
to writing. Without those forerunners, Jane Austen and the
Brontës and George Eliot could no more have written than

Shakespeare could have written without Marlowe, or Marlowe without Chaucer, or Chaucer without those forgotten poets who paved the ways and tamed the natural savagery of the tongue. For masterpieces are not single and solitary births; they are the outcome of many years of thinking in common, of thinking by the body of the people, so that the experience of the mass is behind the single voice. Jane Austen should have laid a wreath upon the grave of Fanny Burney, and George Eliot done homage to the robust shade of Eliza Carter—the valiant old woman who tied a bell to her bedstead in order that she might wake early and learn Greek. All women together ought to let flowers fall upon the tomb of Aphra Behn which is, most scandalously but rather appropriately, in Westminster Abbey, for it was she who earned them the right to speak their minds. It is she—shady and amorous as she was—who makes it not quite fantastic for me to say to you tonight: Earn five hundred a year by your wits.

Here, then, one had reached the early nineteenth century. And here, for the first time, I found several shelves given up entirely to the works of women. But why, I could not help asking, as I ran my eyes over them, were they, with very few exceptions, all novels? The original impulse was to poetry. The "supreme head of song" was a poetess. Both in France and in England the women poets precede the women novelists. Moreover, I thought, looking at the four famous names, what had George Eliot in common with Emily Brontë? Did not Charlotte Brontë fail entirely to understand Jane Austen? Save for the possibly relevant fact that not one of them had a child, four more incongruous characters could not have met together in a room—so much so that it is tempting to invent a meeting and a dialogue between them. Yet by some strange force they were all compelled, when they wrote, to write novels. Had it something to do with being born of the middle class, I asked; and with the fact, which Miss Emily Davies a little later was so strikingly to demonstrate, that the middle-class family in the early nineteenth century was possessed only of a single sitting-room between them? If a woman wrote, she would have to write in the common sitting-room. And, as Miss Nightingale was so vehemently to complain,—"women never have an half hour . . . that they can call their own"—she was always interrupted. Still it would be easier to write prose and fiction there than to write poetry or a play. Less concentration is required. Jane Austen wrote like that to the end of her days. "How she was able to effect all this," her nephew writes in his Memoir, "is surprising, for she had no separate study to repair to, and most of the work must have been done in the general sitting-room, subject to all kinds of casual interruptions. She was careful that her occupation should not be suspected by servants or visitors or any persons beyond her own family party."[1] Jane Austen hid her manuscripts or covered them with a piece of blotting-paper. Then, again, all the literary training that a woman had in the early nineteenth century was training in the observation of character, in the analysis of emotion. Her sensibility had been educated for centuries by the influences of the common sitting-room. People's feelings were impressed on her; personal relations were always before her eyes. Therefore, when the middle-class woman took to writing, she naturally wrote novels, even though, as seems evident enough, two of the four famous women here named were not by nature novelists. Emily Brontë should have written poetic plays; the overflow of George Eliot's capacious mind should have spread itself when the creative impulse was spent upon history or biography. They wrote novels, however; one may even go further, I said, taking *Pride and Prejudice* from the shelf, and say that they wrote good novels. Without boasting or giving

[1] *Memoir of Jane Austen,* by her nephew, James Edward Austen-Leigh.

pain to the opposite sex, one may say that *Pride and Prejudice* is a good book. At any rate, one would not have been ashamed to have been caught in the act of writing *Pride and Prejudice*. Yet Jane Austen was glad that a hinge creaked, so that she might hide her manuscript before anyone came in. To Jane Austen there was something discreditable in writing *Pride and Prejudice*. And, I wondered, would *Pride and Prejudice* have been a better novel if Jane Austen had not thought it necessary to hide her manuscript from visitors? I read a page or two to see; but I could not find any signs that her circumstances had harmed her work in the slightest. That, perhaps, was the chief miracle about it. Here was a woman about the year 1800 writing without hate, without bitterness, without fear, without protest, without preaching. That was how Shakespeare wrote, I thought, looking at *Antony and Cleopatra;* and when people compare Shakespeare and Jane Austen, they may mean that the minds of both had consumed all impediments; and for that reason we do not know Jane Austen and we do not know Shakespeare, and for that reason Jane Austen pervades every word that she wrote, and so does Shakespeare. If Jane Austen suffered in any way from her circumstances it was in the narrowness of life that was imposed upon her. It was impossible for a woman to go about alone. She never travelled; she never drove through London in an omnibus or had luncheon in a shop by herself. But perhaps it was the nature of Jane Austen not to want what she had not. Her gift and her circumstances matched each other completely. But I doubt whether that was true of Charlotte Brontë, I said, opening *Jane Eyre* and laying it beside *Pride and Prejudice.*

I opened it at chapter twelve and my eye was caught by the phrase, "Anybody may blame me who likes." What were they blaming Charlotte Brontë for, I wondered? And I read how Jane Eyre used to go up on to the roof when Mrs. Fairfax was making jellies and looked over the fields at the distant view. And

then she longed—and it was for this that they blamed her—
that "then I longed for a power of vision which might overpass
that limit; which might reach the busy world, towns, regions full
of life I had heard of but never seen: that then I desired more
of practical experience than I possessed; more of intercourse
with my kind, of acquaintance with variety of character than was
here within my reach. I valued what was good in Mrs. Fairfax,
and what was good in Adèle; but I believed in the existence of
other and more vivid kinds of goodness, and what I believed in
I wished to behold.

"Who blames me? Many, no doubt, and I shall be called dis-
contented. I could not help it: the restlessness was in my nature;
it agitated me to pain sometimes. . . .

"It is vain to say human beings ought to be satisfied with
tranquillity: they must have action; and they will make it if they
cannot find it. Millions are condemned to a stiller doom than
mine, and millions are in silent revolt against their lot. Nobody
knows how many rebellions ferment in the masses of life which
people earth. Women are supposed to be very calm generally:
but women feel just as men feel; they need exercise for their faculties and a field for their efforts as much as their brothers do;
they suffer from too rigid a restraint, too absolute a stagnation,
precisely as men would suffer; and it is narrow-minded in their
more privileged fellow-creatures to say that they ought to con-
fine themselves to making puddings and knitting stockings, to
playing on the piano and embroidering bags. It is thoughtless
to condemn them, or laugh at them, if they seek to do more or
learn more than custom has pronounced necessary for their sex.

"When thus alone I not unfrequently heard Grace Poole's
laugh. . . ."

That is an awkward break, I thought. It is upsetting to come
upon Grace Poole all of a sudden. The continuity is disturbed.
One might say, I continued, laying the book down beside *Pride*

and Prejudice, that the woman who wrote those pages had more genius in her than Jane Austen; but if one reads them over and marks that jerk in them, that indignation, one sees that she will never get her genius expressed whole and entire. Her books will be deformed and twisted. She will write in a rage where she should write calmly. She will write foolishly where she should write wisely. She will write of herself where she should write of her characters. She is at war with her lot. How could she help but die young, cramped and thwarted?

One could not but play for a moment with the thought of what might have happened if Charlotte Brontë had possessed say three hundred a year—but the foolish woman sold the copyright of her novels outright for fifteen hundred pounds; had somehow possessed more knowledge of the busy world, and towns and regions full of life; more practical experience, and intercourse with her kind and acquaintance with a variety of character. In those words she puts her finger exactly not only upon her own defects as a novelist but upon those of her sex at that time. She knew, no one better, how enormously her genius would have profited if it had not spent itself in solitary visions over distant fields; if experience and intercourse and travel had been granted her. But they were not granted; they were withheld; and we must accept the fact that all those good novels, *Villette, Emma, Wuthering Heights, Middlemarch,* were written by women without more experience of life than could enter the house of a respectable clergyman; written too in the common sitting-room of that respectable house and by women so poor that they could not afford to buy more than a few quires of paper at a time upon which to write *Wuthering Heights* or *Jane Eyre.* One of them, it is true, George Eliot, escaped after much tribulation, but only to a secluded villa in St. John's Wood. And there she settled down in the shadow of the world's disapproval. "I wish it to be understood," she wrote, "that I should never invite any one to come and see me who did not ask for the invitation"; for was she not living in sin with a married man and might not the sight of her damage the chastity of Mrs. Smith or whoever it might be that chanced to call? One must submit to the social convention, and be "cut off from what is called the world." At the same time, on the other side of Europe, there was a young man living freely with this gipsy or with that great lady; going to the wars; picking up unhindered and uncensored all that varied experience of human life which served him so splendidly later when he came to write his books. Had Tolstoi lived at the Priory in seclusion with a married lady "cut off from what is called the world," however edifying the moral lesson, he could scarcely, I thought, have written *War and Peace*.

But one could perhaps go a little deeper into the question of novel-writing and the effect of sex upon the novelist. If one shuts one's eyes and thinks of the novel as a whole, it would seem to be a creation owning a certain looking-glass likeness to life, though of course with simplifications and distortions innumerable. At any rate, it is a structure leaving a shape on the mind's eye, built now in squares, now pagoda shaped, now throwing out wings and arcades, now solidly compact and domed like the Cathedral of Saint Sofia at Constantinople. This shape, I thought, thinking back over certain famous novels, starts in one the kind of emotion that is appropriate to it. But that emotion at once blends itself with others, for the "shape" is not made by the relation of stone to stone, but by the relation of human being to human being. Thus a novel starts in us all sorts of antagonistic and opposed emotions. Life conflicts with something that is not life. Hence the difficulty of coming to any agreement about novels, and the immense sway that our private prejudices have upon us. On the one hand, we feel You—John the hero—must live, or I shall be in the depths of despair. On the other, we feel, Alas, John, you must die, because the shape of the book requires it. Life conflicts with something that is not life. Then since life it is in part, we judge it as life. James is the sort of man I most detest, one says. Or, This is a farrago of absurdity. I could never feel anything of the sort myself. The whole structure, it is obvious, thinking back on any famous novel, is one of infinite complexity, because it is thus made up of so many different judgments, of so many different kinds of emotion. The wonder is that any book so composed holds together for more than a year or two, or can possibly mean to the English reader what it means for the Russian or the Chinese. But they do hold together occasionally very remarkably. And what holds them together in these rare instances of survival (I was thinking of *War and Peace*) is something that one calls integrity, though it has nothing to do with paying one's bills or behaving honourably in an emergency. What one means by integrity, in the case of the novelist, is the conviction that he gives one that this is the truth. Yes, one feels, I should never have thought that this could be so; I have never known people behaving like that. But you have convinced me that so it is, so it happens. One holds every phrase, every scene to the light as one reads—for Nature seems, very oddly, to have provided us with an inner light by which to judge of the novelist's integrity or disintegrity. Or perhaps it is rather that Nature, in her most irrational mood, has traced in invisible ink on the walls of the mind a premonition which these great artists confirm; a sketch which only needs to be held to the fire of genius to become visible. When one so exposes it and sees it come to life one exclaims in rapture, But this is what I have always felt and known and desired! And one boils over with excitement, and, shutting the book even with a kind of reverence as if it were something very precious, a stand-by to return to as long as one lives, one puts it back on the shelf, I said, taking *War and Peace* and putting it back in its place. If, on the other hand, these poor sentences that one

takes and tests rouse first a quick and eager response with their
bright colouring and their dashing gestures but there they stop:
something seems to check them in their development: or if they
bring to light only a faint scribble in that corner and a blot over
there, and nothing appears whole and entire, then one heaves a
sigh of disappointment and says, Another failure. This novel has
come to grief somewhere.

And for the most part, of course, novels do come to grief
somewhere. The imagination falters under the enormous strain.
The insight is confused; it can no longer distinguish between the
true and the false; it has no longer the strength to go on with
the vast labour that calls at every moment for the use of so
many different faculties. But how would all this be affected by
the sex of the novelist, I wondered, looking at *Jane Eyre* and the
others. Would the fact of her sex in any way interfere with the
integrity of a woman novelist—that integrity which I take to be
the backbone of the writer? Now, in the passages I have quoted
from *Jane Eyre*, it is clear that anger was tampering with the integrity of Charlotte Brontë the novelist. She left her story, to
which her entire devotion was due, to attend to some personal
grievance. She remembered that she had been starved of her
proper due of experience—she had been made to stagnate in a
parsonage mending stockings when she wanted to wander free
over the world. Her imagination swerved from indignation and
we feel it swerve. But there were many more influences than
anger tugging at her imagination and deflecting it from its path.
Ignorance, for instance. The portrait of Rochester is drawn in
the dark. We feel the influence of fear in it; just as we constantly
feel an acidity which is the result of oppression, a buried suffering smouldering beneath her passion, a rancour which contracts
those books, splendid as they are, with a spasm of pain.

And since a novel has this correspondence to real life, its
values are to some extent those of real life. But it is obvious that

the values of women differ very often from the values which have been made by the other sex; naturally, this is so. Yet it is the masculine values that prevail. Speaking crudely, football and sport are "important"; the worship of fashion, the buying of clothes "trivial." And these values are inevitably transferred from life to fiction. This is an important book, the critic assumes, because it deals with war. This is an insignificant book because it deals with the feelings of women in a drawing-room. A scene in a battlefield is more important than a scene in a shop — everywhere and much more subtly the difference of value persists. The whole structure, therefore, of the early nineteenth-century novel was raised, if one was a woman, by a mind which was slightly pulled from the straight, and made to alter its clear vision in deference to external authority. One has only to skim those old forgotten novels and listen to the tone of voice in which they are written to divine that the writer was meeting criticism; she was saying this by way of aggression, or that by way of conciliation. She was admitting that she was "only a woman," or protesting that she was "as good as a man." She met that criticism as her temperament dictated, with docility and diffidence, or with anger and emphasis. It does not matter which it was; she was thinking of something other than the thing itself. Down comes her book upon our heads. There was a flaw in the centre of it. And I thought of all the women's novels that lie scattered, like small pock-marked apples in an orchard, about the second-hand book shops of London. It was the flaw in the centre that had rotted them. She had altered her values in deference to the opinion of others.

But how impossible it must have been for them not to budge either to the right or to the left. What genius, what integrity it must have required in face of all that criticism, in the midst of that purely patriarchal society, to hold fast to the thing as they saw it without shrinking. Only Jane Austen did it and

Emily Brontë. It is another feather, perhaps the finest, in their caps. They wrote as women write, not as men write. Of all the thousand women who wrote novels then, they alone entirely ignored the perpetual admonitions of the eternal pedagogue—write this, think that. They alone were deaf to that persistent voice, now grumbling, now patronising, now domineering, now grieved, now shocked, now angry, now avuncular, that voice which cannot let women alone, but must be at them, like some too conscientious governess, adjuring them, like Sir Egerton Brydges, to be refined; dragging even into the criticism of poetry criticism of sex;[2] admonishing them, if they would be good and win, as I suppose, some shiny prize, to keep within certain limits which the gentleman in question thinks suitable: ". . . female novelists should only aspire to excellence by courageously acknowledging the limitations of their sex."[3] That puts the matter in a nutshell, and when I tell you, rather to your surprise, that this sentence was written not in August 1828 but in August 1928, you will agree, I think, that however delightful it is to us now, it represents a vast body of opinion—I am not going to stir those old pools, I take only what chance has floated to my feet—that was far more vigorous and far more vocal a century ago. It would have needed a very stalwart young woman in 1828 to disregard all those snubs and chidings and promises of prizes. One must have been something of a firebrand to say to oneself, Oh, but they can't buy literature too. Literature is open to everybody. I refuse to allow you, Beadle though you are, to turn me

[2]"[She] has a metaphysical purpose, and that is a dangerous obsession, especially with a woman, for women rarely possess men's healthy love of rhetoric. It is a strange lack in the sex which is in other things more primitive and more materialistic."—*New Criterion,* June 1928.

[3]"If, like the reporter, you believe that female novelists should only aspire to excellence by courageously acknowledging the limitations of their sex (Jane Austen [has] demonstrated how gracefully this gesture can be accomplished). . . ."—*Life and Letters,* August 1928.

off the grass. Lock up your libraries if you like; but there is no gate, no lock, no bolt that you can set upon the freedom of my mind.

But whatever effect discouragement and criticism had upon their writing—and I believe that they had a very great effect—that was unimportant compared with the other difficulty which faced them (I was still considering those early nineteenth-century novelists) when they came to set their thoughts on paper—that is that they had no tradition behind them, or one so short and partial that it was of little help. For we think back through our mothers if we are women. It is useless to go to the great men writers for help, however much one may go to them for pleasure. Lamb, Browne, Thackeray, Newman, Sterne, Dickens, De Quincey—whoever it may be—never helped a woman yet, though she may have learnt a few tricks of them and adapted them to her use. The weight, the pace, the stride of a man's mind are too unlike her own for her to lift anything substantial from him successfully. The ape is too distant to be sedulous. Perhaps the first thing she would find, setting pen to paper, was that there was no common sentence ready for her use. All the great novelists like Thackeray and Dickens and Balzac have written a natural prose, swift but not slovenly, expressive but not precious, taking their own tint without ceasing to be common property. They have based it on the sentence that was current at the time. The sentence that was current at the beginning of the nineteenth century ran something like this perhaps: "The grandeur of their works was an argument with them, not to stop short, but to proceed. They could have no higher excitement or satisfaction than in the exercise of their art and endless generations of truth and beauty. Success prompts to exertion; and habit facilitates success." That is a man's sentence; behind it one can see Johnson, Gibbon and the rest. It was a sentence that was unsuited for a woman's use. Charlotte

Brontë, with all her splendid gift for prose, stumbled and fell with that clumsy weapon in her hands. George Eliot committed atrocities with it that beggar description. Jane Austen looked at it and laughed at it and devised a perfectly natural, shapely sentence proper for her own use and never departed from it. Thus, with less genius for writing than Charlotte Brontë, she got infinitely more said. Indeed, since freedom and fullness of expression are of the essence of the art, such a lack of tradition, such a scarcity and inadequacy of tools, must have told enormously upon the writing of women. Moreover, a book is not made of sentences laid end to end, but of sentences built, if an image helps, into arcades or domes. And this shape too has been made by men out of their own needs for their own uses. There is no reason to think that the form of the epic or of the poetic play suits a woman any more than the sentence suits her. But all the older forms of literature were hardened and set by the time she became a writer. The novel alone was young enough to be soft in her hands—another reason, perhaps, why she wrote novels. Yet who shall say that even now "the novel" (I give it inverted commas to mark my sense of the words' inadequacy), who shall say that even this most pliable of all forms is rightly shaped for her use? No doubt we shall find her knocking that into shape for herself when she has the free use of her limbs; and providing some new vehicle, not necessarily in verse, for the poetry in her. For it is the poetry that is still denied outlet. And I went on to ponder how a woman nowadays would write a poetic tragedy in five acts—would she use verse—would she not use prose rather?

But these are difficult questions which lie in the twilight of the future. I must leave them, if only because they stimulate me to wander from my subject into trackless forests where I shall be lost and, very likely, devoured by wild beasts. I do not want, and I am sure that you do not want me, to broach that very dismal subject, the future of fiction, so that I will only pause here one moment to draw your attention to the great part which must be played in that future so far as women are concerned by physical conditions. The book has somehow to be adapted to the body, and at a venture one would say that women's books should be shorter, more concentrated, than those of men, and framed so that they do not need long hours of steady and un-interrupted work. For interruptions there will always be. Again, the nerves that feed the brain would seem to differ in men and women, and if you are going to make them work their best and hardest, you must find out what treatment suits them— whether these hours of lectures, for instance, which the monks devised, presumably, hundreds of years ago, suit them—what alternations of work and rest they need, interpreting rest not as doing nothing but as doing something but something that is different; and what should that difference be? All this should be discussed and discovered; all this is part of the question of women and fiction. And yet, I continued, approaching the bookcase again, where shall I find that elaborate study of the psychology of women by a woman? If through their incapacity to play football women are not going to be allowed to practise medicine——

Happily my thoughts were now given another turn.

CHAPTER FIVE

I HAD COME at last, in the course of this rambling, to the shelves which hold books by the living; by women and by men; for there are almost as many books written by women now as by men. Or if that is not yet quite true, if the male is still the voluble sex, it is certainly true that women no longer write novels solely. There are Jane Harrison's books on Greek archaeology; Vernon Lee's books on aesthetics; Gertrude Bell's books on Persia. There are books on all sorts of subjects which a generation ago no woman could have touched. There are poems and plays and criticism; there are histories and biographies, books of travel and books of scholarship and research; there are even a few philosophies and books about science and economics. And though novels predominate, novels themselves may very well have changed from association with books of a different feather. The natural simplicity, the epic age of women's writing, may have gone. Reading and criticism may have given her a wider range, a greater subtlety. The impulse towards autobiography may be spent. She may be beginning to use writing as an art, not as a method of self-expression. Among these new novels one might find an answer to several such questions.

I took down one of them at random. It stood at the very end of the shelf, was called *Life's Adventure,* or some such title, by Mary Carmichael, and was published in this very month of

October. It seems to be her first book, I said to myself, but one must read it as if it were the last volume in a fairly long series, continuing all those other books that I have been glancing at— Lady Winchilsea's poems and Aphra Behn's plays and the novels of the four great novelists. For books continue each other, in spite of our habit of judging them separately. And I must also consider her—this unknown woman—as the descendant of all those other women whose circumstances I have been glancing at and see what she inherits of their characteristics and restrictions. So, with a sigh, because novels so often provide an anodyne and not an antidote, glide one into torpid slumbers instead of rousing one with a burning brand, I settled down with a notebook and a pencil to make what I could of Mary Carmichael's first novel, *Life's Adventure*.

To begin with, I ran my eye up and down the page. I am going to get the hang of her sentences first, I said, before I load my memory with blue eyes and brown and the relationship that there may be between Chloe and Roger. There will be time for that when I have decided whether she has a pen in her hand or a pickaxe. So I tried a sentence or two on my tongue. Soon it was obvious that something was not quite in order. The smooth gliding of sentence after sentence was interrupted. Something tore, something scratched; a single word here and there flashed its torch in my eyes. She was "unhanding" herself as they say in the old plays. She is like a person striking a match that will not light, I thought. But why, I asked her as if she were present, are Jane Austen's sentences not of the right shape for you? Must they all be scrapped because Emma and Mr. Woodhouse are dead? Alas, I sighed, that it should be so. For while Jane Austen breaks from melody to melody as Mozart from song to song, to read this writing was like being out at sea in an open boat. Up one went, down one sank. This terseness, this short-windedness, might mean that she was afraid of something; afraid of being called "sentimental" perhaps; or she remembers that women's writing has been called flowery and so provides a superfluity of thorns; but until I have read a scene with some care, I cannot be sure whether she is being herself or some one else. At any rate, she does not lower one's vitality, I thought, reading more carefully. But she is heaping up too many facts. She will not be able to use half of them in a book of this size. (It was about half the length of *Jane Eyre*.) However, by some means or other she succeeded in getting us all—Roger, Chloe, Olivia, Tony and Mr. Bigham— in a canoe up the river. Wait a moment, I said, leaning back in my chair, I must consider the whole thing more carefully before I go any further.

I am almost sure, I said to myself, that Mary Carmichael is playing a trick on us. For I feel as one feels on a switchback railway when the car, instead of sinking, as one has been led to expect, swerves up again. Mary is tampering with the expected sequence. First she broke the sentence; now she has broken the sequence. Very well, she has every right to do both these things if she does them not for the sake of breaking, but for the sake of creating. Which of the two it is I cannot be sure until she has faced herself with a situation. I will give her every liberty, I said, to choose what that situation shall be; she shall make it of tin cans and old kettles if she likes; but she must convince me that she believes it to be a situation; and then when she has made it she must face it. She must jump. And, determined to do my duty by her as reader if she would do her duty by me as writer, I turned the page and read ... I am sorry to break off so abruptly. Are there no men present? Do you promise me that behind that red curtain over there the figure of Sir Chartres Biron is not concealed? We are all women, you assure me? Then I may tell you that the very next words I read were these— "Chloe liked Olivia ..." Do not start. Do not blush. Let us

admit in the privacy of our own society that these things sometimes happen. Sometimes women do like women.

"Chloe liked Olivia," I read. And then it struck me how immense a change was there. Chloe liked Olivia perhaps for the
first time in literature. Cleopatra did not like Octavia. And how
completely *Antony and Cleopatra* would have been altered had
she done so! As it is, I thought, letting my mind, I am afraid,
wander a little from *Life's Adventure,* the whole thing is simpli-
fied, conventionalised, if one dared say it, absurdly. Cleopatra's
only feeling about Octavia is one of jealousy. Is she taller than
I am? How does she do her hair? The play, perhaps, required
no more. But how interesting it would have been if the relationship between the two women had been more complicated. All
these relationships between women, I thought, rapidly recalling
the splendid gallery of fictitious women, are too simple. So
much has been left out, unattempted. And I tried to remember
any case in the course of my reading where two women are represented as friends. There is an attempt at it in *Diana of the Crossways.* They are confidantes, of course, in Racine and the Greek
tragedies. They are now and then mothers and daughters. But
almost without exception they are shown in their relation to
men. It was strange to think that all the great women of fiction
were, until Jane Austen's day, not only seen by the other sex, but
seen only in relation to the other sex. And how small a part of
a woman's life is that; and how little can a man know even of
that when he observes it through the black or rosy spectacles
which sex puts upon his nose. Hence, perhaps, the peculiar nature of woman in fiction; the astonishing extremes of her beauty
and horror; her alternations between heavenly goodness and
hellish depravity—for so a lover would see her as his love rose
or sank, was prosperous or unhappy. This is not so true of the
nineteenth-century novelists, of course. Woman becomes much

more various and complicated there. Indeed it was the desire to write about women perhaps that led men by degrees to abandon the poetic drama which, with its violence, could make so little use of them, and to devise the novel as a more fitting receptacle. Even so it remains obvious, even in the writing of Proust, that a man is terribly hampered and partial in his knowledge of women, as a woman in her knowledge of men.

Also, I continued, looking down at the page again, it is becoming evident that women, like men, have other interests besides the perennial interests of domesticity. "Chloe liked Olivia. They shared a laboratory together. . . ." I read on and discovered that these two young women were engaged in mincing liver, which is, it seems, a cure for pernicious anaemia: although one of them was married and had—I think I am right in stating—two small children. Now all that, of course, has had to be left out, and thus the splendid portrait of the fictitious woman is much too simple and much too monotonous. Suppose, for instance, that men were only represented in literature as the lovers of women, and were never the friends of men, soldiers, thinkers, dreamers; how few parts in the plays of Shakespeare could be allotted to them; how literature would suffer! We might perhaps have most of Othello; and a good deal of Antony; but no Caesar, no Brutus, no Hamlet, no Lear, no Jaques—literature would be incredibly impoverished, as indeed literature is impoverished beyond our counting by the doors that have been shut upon women. Married against their will, kept in one room, and to one occupation, how could a dramatist give a full or interesting or truthful account of them? Love was the only possible interpreter. The poet was forced to be passionate or bitter, unless indeed he chose to "hate women," which meant more often than not that he was unattractive to them.

Now if Chloe likes Olivia and they share a laboratory, which of itself will make their friendship more varied and lasting because it will be less personal; if Mary Carmichael knows how to write, and I was beginning to enjoy some quality in her style; if she has a room to herself, of which I am not quite sure; if she has five hundred a year of her own—but that remains to be proved—then I think that something of great importance has happened.

For if Chloe likes Olivia and Mary Carmichael knows how to express it she will light a torch in that vast chamber where nobody has yet been. It is all half lights and profound shadows like those serpentine caves where one goes with a candle peering up and down, not knowing where one is stepping. And I began to read the book again, and read how Chloe watched Olivia put a jar on a shelf and say how it was time to go home to her children. That is a sight that has never been seen since the world began, I exclaimed. And I watched too, very curiously. For I wanted to see how Mary Carmichael set to work to catch those unrecorded gestures, those unsaid or half-said words, which form themselves, no more palpably than the shadows of moths on the ceiling, when women are alone, unlit by the capricious and coloured light of the other sex. She will need to hold her breath, I said, reading on, if she is to do it; for women are so suspicious of any interest that has not some obvious motive behind it, so terribly accustomed to concealment and suppression, that they are off at the flicker of an eye turned observingly in their direction. The only way for you to do it, I thought, addressing Mary Carmichael as if she were there, would be to talk of something else, looking steadily out of the window, and thus note, not with a pencil in a notebook, but in the shortest of shorthand, in words that are hardly syllabled yet, what happens when Olivia—this organism that has been under the shadow of the rock these million years—feels the light fall on it, and sees coming her way a piece of strange food—knowledge, adventure, art. And she reaches out for it, I thought, again raising my

eyes from the page, and has to devise some entirely new com-
bination of her resources, so highly developed for other purposes, so as to absorb the new into the old without disturbing
the infinitely intricate and elaborate balance of the whole.

But, alas, I had done what I had determined not to do; I had
slipped unthinkingly into praise of my own sex. "Highly developed"—"infinitely intricate"—such are undeniably terms of
praise, and to praise one's own sex is always suspect, often silly;
moreover, in this case, how could one justify it? One could not
go to the map and say Columbus discovered America and
Columbus was a woman; or take an apple and remark, Newton
discovered the laws of gravitation and Newton was a woman;
or look into the sky and say aeroplanes are flying overhead and
aeroplanes were invented by women. There is no mark on the
wall to measure the precise height of women. There are no yard
measures, neatly divided into the fractions of an inch, that one
can lay against the qualities of a good mother or the devotion
of a daughter, or the fidelity of a sister, or the capacity of a
housekeeper. Few women even now have been graded at the
universities; the great trials of the professions, army and navy,
trade, politics and diplomacy have hardly tested them. They remain even at this moment almost unclassified. But if I want to
know all that a human being can tell me about Sir Hawley Butts,
for instance, I have only to open Burke or Debrett and I shall
find that he took such and such a degree; owns a hall; has an
heir; was Secretary to a Board; represented Great Britain in
Canada; and has received a certain number of degrees, offices,
medals and other distinctions by which his merits are stamped
upon him indelibly. Only Providence can know more about Sir
Hawley Butts than that.

When, therefore, I say "highly developed," "infinitely intricate," of women, I am unable to verify my words either in
Whitaker, Debrett or the University Calendar. In this predica-

ment what can I do? And I looked at the bookcase again. There were the biographies: Johnson and Goethe and Carlyle and Sterne and Cowper and Shelley and Voltaire and Browning and many others. And I began thinking of all those great men who have for one reason or another admired, sought out, lived with, confided in, made love to, written of, trusted in, and shown what can only be described as some need of and dependence upon certain persons of the opposite sex. That all these relationships were absolutely Platonic I would not affirm, and Sir William Joynson Hicks would probably deny. But we should wrong these illustrious men very greatly if we insisted that they got nothing from these alliances but comfort, flattery and the pleasures of the body. What they got, it is obvious, was something that their own sex was unable to supply; and it would not be rash, perhaps, to define it further, without quoting the doubtless rhapsodical words of the poets, as some stimulus, some renewal of creative power which is in the gift only of the opposite sex to bestow. He would open the door of drawing-room or nursery, I thought, and find her among her children perhaps, or with a piece of embroidery on her knee—at any rate, the centre of some different order and system of life, and the contrast between this world and his own, which might be the law courts or the House of Commons, would at once refresh and invigorate; and there would follow, even in the simplest talk, such a natural difference of opinion that the dried ideas in him would be fertilised anew; and the sight of her creating in a different medium from his own would so quicken his creative power that insensibly his sterile mind would begin to plot again, and he would find the phrase or the scene which was lacking when he put on his hat to visit her. Every Johnson has his Thrale, and holds fast to her for some such reasons as these, and when the Thrale marries her Italian music master Johnson goes half mad with rage and disgust, not merely that he will miss his pleasant

evenings at Streatham, but that the light of his life will be "as if
gone out."

And without being Dr. Johnson or Goethe or Carlyle or
Voltaire, one may feel, though very differently from these great
men, the nature of this intricacy and the power of this highly developed creative faculty among women. One goes into the
room—but the resources of the English language would be
much put to the stretch, and whole flights of words would need
to wing their way illegitimately into existence before a woman
could say what happens when she goes into a room. The rooms
differ so completely; they are calm or thunderous; open on to
the sea, or, on the contrary, give on to a prison yard; are hung
with washing; or alive with opals and silks; are hard as horsehair
or soft as feathers—one has only to go into any room in any
street for the whole of that extremely complex force of femi-
ninity to fly in one's face. How should it be otherwise? For
women have sat indoors all these millions of years, so that by
this time the very walls are permeated by their creative force,
which has, indeed, so overcharged the capacity of bricks and
mortar that it must needs harness itself to pens and brushes and
business and politics. But this creative power differs greatly
from the creative power of men. And one must conclude that it
would be a thousand pities if it were hindered or wasted, for it
was won by centuries of the most drastic discipline, and there is
nothing to take its place. It would be a thousand pities if women
wrote like men, or lived like men, or looked like men, for if two
sexes are quite inadequate, considering the vastness and variety
of the world, how should we manage with one only? Ought not
education to bring out and fortify the differences rather than
the similarities? For we have too much likeness as it is, and if an
explorer should come back and bring word of other sexes looking through the branches of other trees at other skies, nothing
would be of greater service to humanity; and we should have

the immense pleasure into the bargain of watching Professor X rush for his measuring-rods to prove himself "superior."

Mary Carmichael, I thought, still hovering at a little distance above the page, will have her work cut out for her merely as an observer. I am afraid indeed that she will be tempted to become, what I think the less interesting branch of the species— the naturalist-novelist, and not the contemplative. There are so many new facts for her to observe. She will not need to limit herself any longer to the respectable houses of the upper middle classes. She will go without kindness or condescension, but in the spirit of fellowship into those small, scented rooms where sit the courtesan, the harlot and the lady with the pug dog. There they still sit in the rough and ready-made clothes that the male writer has had perforce to clap upon their shoulders. But Mary Carmichael will have out her scissors and fit them close to every hollow and angle. It will be a curious sight, when it comes, to see these women as they are, but we must wait a little, for Mary Carmichael will still be encumbered with that self-consciousness in the presence of "sin" which is the legacy of our sexual barbarity. She will still wear the shoddy old fetters of class on her feet.

However, the majority of women are neither harlots nor courtesans; nor do they sit clasping pug dogs to dusty velvet all through the summer afternoon. But what do they do then? and there came to my mind's eye one of those long streets somewhere south of the river whose infinite rows are innumerably populated. With the eye of the imagination I saw a very ancient lady crossing the street on the arm of a middle-aged woman, her daughter, perhaps, both so respectably booted and furred that their dressing in the afternoon must be a ritual, and the clothes themselves put away in cupboards with camphor, year after year, throughout the summer months. They cross the road when the lamps are being lit (for the dusk is their favourite hour), as they

must have done year after year. The elder is close on eighty; but
if one asked her what her life has meant to her, she would say
that she remembered the streets lit for the battle of Balaclava,
or had heard the guns fire in Hyde Park for the birth of King
Edward the Seventh. And if one asked her, longing to pin down
the moment with date and season, but what were you doing on
the fifth of April 1868, or the second of November 1875, she
would look vague and say that she could remember nothing. For
all the dinners are cooked; the plates and cups washed; the children sent to school and gone out into the world. Nothing remains of it all. All has vanished. No biography or history has a
word to say about it. And the novels, without meaning to, inevitably lie.

All these infinitely obscure lives remain to be recorded, I
said, addressing Mary Carmichael as if she were present; and
went on in thought through the streets of London feeling
in imagination the pressure of dumbness, the accumulation of
unrecorded life, whether from the women at the street corners
with their arms akimbo, and the rings embedded in their fat
swollen fingers, talking with a gesticulation like the swing of
Shakespeare's words; or from the violet-sellers and match-
sellers and old crones stationed under doorways; or from drifting girls whose faces, like waves in sun and cloud, signal the
coming of men and women and the flickering lights of shop
windows. All that you will have to explore, I said to Mary Carmichael, holding your torch firm in your hand. Above all,
you must illumine your own soul with its profundities and its
shallows, and its vanities and its generosities, and say what your
beauty means to you or your plainness, and what is your relation to the everchanging and turning world of gloves and shoes
and stuffs swaying up and down among the faint scents that
come through chemists' bottles down arcades of dress material
over a floor of pseudo-marble. For in imagination I had gone

into a shop; it was laid with black and white paving; it was hung, astonishingly beautifully, with coloured ribbons. Mary Carmichael might well have a look at that in passing, I thought, for it is a sight that would lend itself to the pen as fittingly as any snowy peak or rocky gorge in the Andes. And there is the girl behind the counter too — I would as soon have her true history as the hundred and fiftieth life of Napoleon or seventieth study of Keats and his use of Miltonic inversion which old Professor Z and his like are now inditing. And then I went on very warily, on the very tips of my toes (so cowardly am I, so afraid of the lash that was once almost laid on my own shoulders), to murmur that she should also learn to laugh, without bitterness, at the vanities — say rather at the peculiarities, for it is a less offensive word — of the other sex. For there is a spot the size of a shilling at the back of the head which one can never see for oneself. It is one of the good offices that sex can discharge for sex — to describe that spot the size of a shilling at the back of the head. Think how much women have profited by the comments of Juvenal; by the criticism of Strindberg. Think with what humanity and brilliancy men, from the earliest ages, have pointed out to women that dark place at the back of the head! And if Mary were very brave and very honest, she would go behind the other sex and tell us what she found there. A true picture of man as a whole can never be painted until a woman has described that spot the size of a shilling. Mr. Woodhouse and Mr. Casaubon are spots of that size and nature. Not of course that any one in their senses would counsel her to hold up to scorn and ridicule of set purpose — literature shows the futility of what is written in that spirit. Be truthful, one would say, and the result is bound to be amazingly interesting. Comedy is bound to be enriched. New facts are bound to be discovered.

However, it was high time to lower my eyes to the page again. It would be better, instead of speculating what Mary

Carmichael might write and should write, to see what in fact
Mary Carmichael did write. So I began to read again. I remembered that I had certain grievances against her. She had broken
up Jane Austen's sentence, and thus given me no chance of
pluming myself upon my impeccable taste, my fastidious ear.
For it was useless to say, "Yes, yes, this is very nice; but Jane
Austen wrote much better than you do," when I had to admit
that there was no point of likeness between them. Then she had
gone further and broken the sequence—the expected order.
Perhaps she had done this unconsciously, merely giving things
their natural order, as a woman would, if she wrote like a woman.
But the effect was somehow baffling; one could not see a wave
heaping itself, a crisis coming round the next corner. Therefore
I could not plume myself either upon the depths of my feelings
and my profound knowledge of the human heart. For whenever
I was about to feel the usual things in the usual places, about
love, about death, the annoying creature twitched me away, as
if the important point were just a little further on. And thus
she made it impossible for me to roll out my sonorous phrases
about "elemental feelings," the "common stuff of humanity,"
"depths of the human heart," and all those other phrases which
support us in our belief that, however clever we may be on top,
we are very serious, very profound and very humane under-
neath. She made me feel, on the contrary, that instead of being
serious and profound and humane, one might be—and the
thought was far less seductive—merely lazy minded and conventional into the bargain.

But I read on, and noted certain other facts. She was no
"genius"—that was evident. She had nothing like the love of
Nature, the fiery imagination, the wild poetry, the brilliant wit,
the brooding wisdom of her great predecessors, Lady Winchilsea,
Charlotte Brontë, Emily Brontë, Jane Austen and George Eliot;
she could not write with the melody and the dignity of Dorothy

Osborne—indeed she was no more than a clever girl whose books will no doubt be pulped by the publishers in ten years' time. But, nevertheless, she had certain advantages which women of far greater gift lacked even half a century ago. Men were no longer to her "the opposing faction"; she need not waste her time railing against them; she need not climb on to the roof and ruin her peace of mind longing for travel, experience and a knowledge of the world and character that were denied her. Fear and hatred were almost gone, or traces of them showed only in a slight exaggeration of the joy of freedom, a tendency to the caustic and satirical, rather than to the romantic, in her treatment of the other sex. Then there could be no doubt that as a novelist she enjoyed some natural advantages of a high order. She had a sensibility that was very wide, eager and free. It responded to an almost imperceptible touch on it. It feasted like a plant newly stood in the air on every sight and sound that came its way. It ranged, too, very subtly and curiously, among almost unknown or unrecorded things; it lighted on small things and showed that perhaps they were not small after all. It brought buried things to light and made one wonder what need there had been to bury them. Awkward though she was and without the unconscious bearing of long descent which makes the least turn of the pen of a Thackeray or a Lamb delightful to the ear, she had—I began to think—mastered the first great lesson; she wrote as a woman, but as a woman who has forgotten that she is a woman, so that her pages were full of that curious sexual quality which comes only when sex is unconscious of itself.

All this was to the good. But no abundance of sensation or fineness of perception would avail unless she could build up out of the fleeting and the personal the lasting edifice which remains unthrown. I had said that I would wait until she faced herself with "a situation." And I meant by that until she proved

by summoning, beckoning and getting together that she was
not a skimmer of surfaces merely, but had looked beneath into
the depths. Now is the time, she would say to herself at a certain moment, when without doing anything violent I can show
the meaning of all this. And she would begin—how unmistak-
able that quickening is!—beckoning and summoning, and there
would rise up in memory, half forgotten, perhaps quite trivial
things in other chapters dropped by the way. And she would
make their presence felt while some one sewed or smoked a
pipe as naturally as possible, and one would feel, as she went on
writing, as if one had gone to the top of the world and seen it
laid out, very majestically, beneath.

At any rate, she was making the attempt. And as I watched
her lengthening out for the test, I saw, but hoped that she did
not see, the bishops and the deans, the doctors and the professors, the patriarchs and the pedagogues all at her shouting warning and advice. You can't do this and you shan't do that! Fellows
and scholars only allowed on the grass! Ladies not admitted
without a letter of introduction! Aspiring and graceful female
novelists this way! So they kept at her like the crowd at a fence
on the race-course, and it was her trial to take her fence without looking to right or left. If you stop to curse you are lost, I
said to her; equally, if you stop to laugh. Hesitate or fumble and
you are done for. Think only of the jump, I implored her, as if
I had put the whole of my money on her back; and she went
over it like a bird. But there was a fence beyond that and a fence
beyond that. Whether she had the staying power I was doubtful, for the clapping and the crying were fraying to the nerves.
But she did her best. Considering that Mary Carmichael was no
genius, but an unknown girl writing her first novel in a bed-
sitting-room, without enough of those desirable things, time,
money and idleness, she did not do so badly, I thought.

Give her another hundred years, I concluded, reading the last chapter—people's noses and bare shoulders showed naked against a starry sky, for some one had twitched the curtain in the drawing-room—give her a room of her own and five hundred a year, let her speak her mind and leave out half that she now puts in, and she will write a better book one of these days. She will be a poet, I said, putting *Life's Adventure*, by Mary Carmichael, at the end of the shelf, in another hundred years' time.

CHAPTER SIX

NEXT DAY the light of the October morning was falling in dusty shafts through the uncurtained windows, and the hum of traffic rose from the street. London then was winding itself up again; the factory was astir; the machines were beginning. It was tempting, after all this reading, to look out of the window and see what London was doing on the morning of the twenty-sixth of October 1928. And what was London doing? Nobody, it seemed, was reading *Antony and Cleopatra*. London was wholly indifferent, it appeared, to Shakespeare's plays. Nobody cared a straw—and I do not blame them—for the future of fiction, the death of poetry or the development by the average woman of a prose style completely expressive of her mind. If opinions upon any of these matters had been chalked on the pavement, nobody would have stooped to read them. The nonchalance of the hurrying feet would have rubbed them out in half an hour. Here came an errand-boy; here a woman with a dog on a lead. The fascination of the London street is that no two people are ever alike; each seems bound on some private affair of his own. There were the business-like, with their little bags; there were the drifters rattling sticks upon area railings; there were affable characters to whom the streets serve for clubroom, hailing men in carts and giving information without being asked for it. Also there were funerals to which men, thus suddenly reminded of the passing of their own bodies, lifted their hats. And then a very distinguished gentleman came slowly down a doorstep and paused to avoid collision with a bustling lady who had, by some means or other, acquired a splendid fur coat and a bunch of Parma violets. They all seemed separate, self-absorbed, on business of their own.

At this moment, as so often happens in London, there was a complete lull and suspension of traffic. Nothing came down the street; nobody passed. A single leaf detached itself from the plane tree at the end of the street, and in that pause and suspension fell. Somehow it was like a signal falling, a signal pointing to a force in things which one had overlooked. It seemed to point to a river, which flowed past, invisibly, round the corner, down the street, and took people and eddied them along, as the stream at Oxbridge had taken the undergraduate in his boat and the dead leaves. Now it was bringing from one side of the street to the other diagonally a girl in patent leather boots, and then a young man in a maroon overcoat; it was also bringing a taxi-cab; and it brought all three together at a point directly beneath my window; where the taxi stopped; and the girl and the young man stopped; and they got into the taxi; and then the cab glided off as if it were swept on by the current elsewhere.

The sight was ordinary enough; what was strange was the rhythmical order with which my imagination had invested it; and the fact that the ordinary sight of two people getting into a cab had the power to communicate something of their own seeming satisfaction. The sight of two people coming down the street and meeting at the corner seems to ease the mind of some strain, I thought, watching the taxi turn and make off. Perhaps to think, as I had been thinking these two days, of one sex as distinct from the other is an effort. It interferes with the unity of the mind. Now that effort had ceased and that unity had been restored by seeing two people come together and get into

a taxi-cab. The mind is certainly a very mysterious organ, I reflected, drawing my head in from the window, about which
nothing whatever is known, though we depend upon it so completely. Why do I feel that there are severances and oppositions
in the mind, as there are strains from obvious causes on the
body? What does one mean by "the unity of the mind," I pondered, for clearly the mind has so great a power of concentrat-
ing at any point at any moment that it seems to have no single
state of being. It can separate itself from the people in the street,
for example, and think of itself as apart from them, at an upper
window looking down on them. Or it can think with other
people spontaneously, as, for instance, in a crowd waiting to
hear some piece of news read out. It can think back through its
fathers or through its mothers, as I have said that a woman writing thinks back through her mothers. Again if one is a woman
one is often surprised by a sudden splitting off of consciousness, say in walking down Whitehall, when from being the natural inheritor of that civilisation, she becomes, on the contrary,
outside of it, alien and critical. Clearly the mind is always altering its focus, and bringing the world into different perspectives.
But some of these states of mind seem, even if adopted spontaneously, to be less comfortable than others. In order to keep
oneself continuing in them one is unconsciously holding something back, and gradually the repression becomes an effort. But
there may be some state of mind in which one could continue
without effort because nothing is required to be held back. And
this perhaps, I thought, coming in from the window, is one of
them. For certainly when I saw the couple get into the taxi-cab
the mind felt as if, after being divided, it had come together
again in a natural fusion. The obvious reason would be that it is
natural for the sexes to co-operate. One has a profound, if irrational, instinct in favour of the theory that the union of man and
woman makes for the greatest satisfaction, the most complete

happiness. But the sight of the two people getting into the taxi and the satisfaction it gave me made me also ask whether there are two sexes in the mind corresponding to the two sexes in the body, and whether they also require to be united in order to get complete satisfaction and happiness. And I went on amateurishly to sketch a plan of the soul so that in each of us two powers preside, one male, one female; and in the man's brain the man predominates over the woman, and in the woman's brain, the woman predominates over the man. The normal and comfortable state of being is that when the two live in harmony together, spiritually co-operating. If one is a man, still the woman part of his brain must have effect; and a woman also must have intercourse with the man in her. Coleridge perhaps meant this when he said that a great mind is androgynous. It is when this fusion takes place that the mind is fully fertilised and uses all its faculties. Perhaps a mind that is purely masculine cannot create, any more than a mind that is purely feminine, I thought. But it would be well to test what one meant by man-womanly, and conversely by woman-manly, by pausing and looking at a book or two.

Coleridge certainly did not mean, when he said that a great mind is androgynous, that it is a mind that has any special sympathy with women; a mind that takes up their cause or devotes itself to their interpretation. Perhaps the androgynous mind is less apt to make these distinctions than the single-sexed mind. He meant, perhaps, that the androgynous mind is resonant and porous; that it transmits emotion without impediment; that it is naturally creative, incandescent and undivided. In fact one goes back to Shakespeare's mind as the type of the androgynous, of the man-womanly mind, though it would be impossible to say what Shakespeare thought of women. And if it be true that it is one of the tokens of the fully developed mind that it does not think specially or separately of sex, how much harder it is to attain that condition now than ever before. Here I came to the books by living writers, and there paused and wondered if this fact were not at the root of something that had long puzzled me. No age can ever have been as stridently sex-conscious as our own; those innumerable books by men about women in the British Museum are a proof of it. The Suffrage campaign was no doubt to blame. It must have roused in men an extraordinary desire for self-assertion; it must have made them lay an emphasis upon their own sex and its characteristics which they would not have troubled to think about had they not been challenged. And when one is challenged, even by a few women in black bonnets, one retaliates, if one has never been challenged before, rather excessively. That perhaps accounts for some of the characteristics that I remember to have found here, I thought, taking down a new novel by Mr. A, who is in the prime of life and very well thought of, apparently, by the reviewers. I opened it. Indeed, it was delightful to read a man's writing again. It was so direct, so straightforward after the writing of women. It indicated such freedom of mind, such liberty of person, such confidence in himself. One had a sense of physical well-being in the presence of this well-nourished, well-educated, free mind, which had never been thwarted or opposed, but had had full liberty from birth to stretch itself in whatever way it liked. All this was admirable. But after reading a chapter or two a shadow seemed to lie across the page. It was a straight dark bar, a shadow shaped something like the letter "I." One began dodging this way and that to catch a glimpse of the landscape behind it. Whether that was indeed a tree or a woman walking I was not quite sure. Back one was always hailed to the letter "I." One began to be tired of "I." Not but what this "I" was a most respectable "I"; honest and logical; as hard as a nut, and polished for centuries by good teaching and good feeding. I respect and admire that "I" from the bottom of my heart. But—here I turned a page or two, looking for something or other—the worst of it is that in the shadow of the letter "I" all is shapeless as mist. Is that a tree? No, it is a woman. But . . . she has not a bone in her body, I thought, watching Phoebe, for that was her name, coming across the beach. Then Alan got up and the shadow of Alan at once obliterated Phoebe. For Alan had views and Phoebe was quenched in the flood of his views. And then Alan, I thought, has passions; and here I turned page after page very fast, feeling that the crisis was approaching, and so it was. It took place on the beach under the sun. It was done very openly. It was done very vigorously. Nothing could have been more indecent. But . . . I had said "but" too often. One cannot go on saying "but." One must finish the sentence somehow, I rebuked myself. Shall I finish it, "But—I am bored!" But why was I bored? Partly because of the dominance of the letter "I" and the aridity, which, like the giant beech tree, it casts within its shade. Nothing will grow there. And partly for some more obscure reason. There seemed to be some obstacle, some impediment in Mr. A's mind which blocked the fountain of creative energy and shored it within narrow limits. And remembering the lunch party at Oxbridge, and the cigarette ash and the Manx cat and Tennyson and Christina Rossetti all in a bunch, it seemed possible that the impediment lay there. As he no longer hums under his breath, "There has fallen a splendid tear from the passion-flower at the gate," when Phoebe crosses the beach, and she no longer replies, "My heart is like a singing bird whose nest is in a water'd shoot," when Alan approaches what can he do? Being honest as the day and logical as the sun, there is only one thing he can do. And that he does, to do him justice, over and over (I said, turning the pages) and over again. And that, I added, aware of the awful nature of the confession, seems somehow dull. Shakespeare's indecency uproots a thousand other things in one's mind, and is far from being dull. But Shakespeare does it for pleasure; Mr. A, as the nurses say, does it on purpose. He does it in protest. He is protesting against the equality of the other sex by asserting his own superiority. He is therefore impeded and inhibited and self-conscious as Shakespeare might have been if he too had known Miss Clough and Miss Davies. Doubtless Elizabethan literature would have been very different from what it is if the woman's movement had begun in the sixteenth century and not in the nineteenth.

What, then, it amounts to, if this theory of the two sides of the mind holds good, is that virility has now become self-conscious—men, that is to say, are now writing only with the male side of their brains. It is a mistake for a woman to read them, for she will inevitably look for something that she will not find. It is the power of suggestion that one most misses, I thought, taking Mr. B the critic in my hand and reading, very carefully and very dutifully, his remarks upon the art of poetry. Very able they were, acute and full of learning; but the trouble was, that his feelings no longer communicated; his mind seemed separated into different chambers; not a sound carried from one to the other. Thus, when one takes a sentence of Mr. B into the mind it falls plump to the ground—dead; but when one takes a sentence of Coleridge into the mind, it explodes and gives birth to all kinds of other ideas, and that is the only sort of writing of which one can say that it has the secret of perpetual life.

But whatever the reason may be, it is a fact that one must deplore. For it means—here I had come to rows of books by Mr. Galsworthy and Mr. Kipling—that some of the finest works of our greatest living writers fall upon deaf ears. Do what she will a woman cannot find in them that fountain of perpetual life which the critics assure her is there. It is not only that they celebrate male virtues, enforce male values and describe the world of men; it is that the emotion with which these books are permeated is to a woman incomprehensible. It is coming, it is gathering, it is about to burst on one's head, one begins saying long before the end. That picture will fall on old Jolyon's head; he will die of the shock; the old clerk will speak over him two or three obituary words; and all the swans on the Thames will simultaneously burst out singing. But one will rush away before that happens and hide in the gooseberry bushes, for the emotion which is so deep, so subtle, so symbolical to a man moves a woman to wonder. So with Mr. Kipling's officers who turn their backs; and his Sowers who sow the Seed; and his Men who are alone with their Work; and the Flag—one blushes at all these capital letters as if one had been caught eavesdropping at some purely masculine orgy. The fact is that neither Mr. Galsworthy nor Mr. Kipling has a spark of the woman in him. Thus all their qualities seem to a woman, if one may generalise, crude and immature. They lack suggestive power. And when a book lacks suggestive power, however hard it hits the surface of the mind it cannot penetrate within.

And in that restless mood in which one takes books out and puts them back again without looking at them I began to envisage an age to come of pure, of self-assertive virility, such as the letters of professors (take Sir Walter Raleigh's letters, for instance) seem to forebode, and the rulers of Italy have already brought into being. For one can hardly fail to be impressed in Rome by the sense of unmitigated masculinity; and whatever the value of unmitigated masculinity upon the state, one may question the effect of it upon the art of poetry. At any rate, according to the newspapers, there is a certain anxiety about fiction in Italy. There has been a meeting of academicians whose object it is "to develop the Italian novel." "Men famous by birth, or in finance, industry or the Fascist corporations" came together the other day and discussed the matter, and a telegram was sent to the Duce expressing the hope "that the Fascist era would soon give birth to a poet worthy of it." We may all join

in that pious hope, but it is doubtful whether poetry can come
out of an incubator. Poetry ought to have a mother as well as a
father. The Fascist poem, one may fear, will be a horrid little
abortion such as one sees in a glass jar in the museum of some
county town. Such monsters never live long, it is said; one has
never seen a prodigy of that sort cropping grass in a field. Two
heads on one body do not make for length of life.

However, the blame for all this, if one is anxious to lay
blame, rests no more upon one sex than upon the other. All
seducers and reformers are responsible, Lady Bessborough
when she lied to Lord Granville; Miss Davies when she told the
truth to Mr. Greg. All who have brought about a state of sex-
consciousness are to blame, and it is they who drive me, when
I want to stretch my faculties on a book, to seek it in that happy
age, before Miss Davies and Miss Clough were born, when the
writer used both sides of his mind equally. One must turn back
to Shakespeare then, for Shakespeare was androgynous; and so
was Keats and Sterne and Cowper and Lamb and Coleridge.
Shelley perhaps was sexless. Milton and Ben Jonson had a dash
too much of the male in them. So had Wordsworth and Tolstoi.
In our time Proust was wholly androgynous, if not perhaps a
little too much of a woman. But that failing is too rare for one
to complain of it, since without some mixture of the kind the
intellect seems to predominate and the other faculties of the
mind harden and become barren. However, I consoled myself
with the reflection that this is perhaps a passing phase; much of
what I have said in obedience to my promise to give you the
course of my thoughts will seem out of date; much of what
flames in my eyes will seem dubious to you who have not yet
come of age.

Even so, the very first sentence that I would write here, I
said, crossing over to the writing-table and taking up the page
headed Women and Fiction, is that it is fatal for any one who

writes to think of their sex. It is fatal to be a man or woman pure and simple; one must be woman-manly or man-womanly. It is fatal for a woman to lay the least stress on any grievance; to plead even with justice any cause; in any way to speak consciously as a woman. And fatal is no figure of speech; for anything written with that conscious bias is doomed to death. It ceases to be fertilised. Brilliant and effective, powerful and masterly, as it may appear for a day or two, it must wither at nightfall; it cannot grow in the minds of others. Some collaboration has to take place in the mind between the woman and the man before the act of creation can be accomplished. Some marriage of opposites has to be consummated. The whole of the mind must lie wide open if we are to get the sense that the writer is communicating his experience with perfect fullness. There must be freedom and there must be peace. Not a wheel must grate, not a light glimmer. The curtains must be close drawn. The writer, I thought, once his experience is over, must lie back and let his mind celebrate its nuptials in darkness. He must not look or question what is being done. Rather, he must pluck the petals from a rose or watch the swans float calmly down the river. And I saw again the current which took the boat and the undergraduate and the dead leaves; and the taxi took the man and the woman, I thought, seeing them come together across the street, and the current swept them away, I thought, hearing far off the roar of London's traffic, into that tremendous stream.

HERE, THEN, Mary Beton ceases to speak. She has told you how she reached the conclusion—the prosaic conclusion—that it is necessary to have five hundred a year and a room with a lock on the door if you are to write fiction or poetry. She has tried to lay bare the thoughts and impressions that led her to think this. She has asked you to follow her flying into the arms of a Beadle, lunching here, dining there, drawing pictures in the

British Museum, taking books from the shelf, looking out of the window. While she has been doing all these things, you no doubt have been observing her failings and foibles and deciding what effect they have had on her opinions. You have been contradicting her and making whatever additions and deductions seem good to you. That is all as it should be, for in a question like this truth is only to be had by laying together many varieties of error. And I will end now in my own person by anticipating two criticisms, so obvious that you can hardly fail to make them.

No opinion has been expressed, you may say, upon the comparative merits of the sexes even as writers. That was done purposely, because, even if the time had come for such a valuation—and it is far more important at the moment to know how much money women had and how many rooms than to theorise about their capacities—even if the time had come I do not believe that gifts, whether of mind or character, can be weighed like sugar and butter, not even in Cambridge, where they are so adept at putting people into classes and fixing caps on their heads and letters after their names. I do not believe that even the Table of Precedency which you will find in Whitaker's *Almanac* represents a final order of values, or that there is any sound reason to suppose that a Commander of the Bath will ultimately walk in to dinner behind a Master in Lunacy. All this pitting of sex against sex, of quality against quality; all this claiming of superiority and imputing of inferiority, belong to the private-school stage of human existence where there are "sides," and it is necessary for one side to beat another side, and of the utmost importance to walk up to a platform and receive from the hands of the Headmaster himself a highly ornamental pot. As people mature they cease to believe in sides or in Headmasters or in highly ornamental pots. At any rate, where books are concerned, it is notoriously difficult to fix labels of merit in such a way that they do not come off. Are not reviews of current literature a perpetual illustration of the difficulty of judgment? "This great book," "this worthless book," the same book is called by both names. Praise and blame alike mean nothing. No, delightful as the pastime of measuring may be, it is the most futile of all occupations, and to submit to the decrees of the measurers the most servile of attitudes. So long as you write what you wish to write, that is all that matters; and whether it matters for ages or only for hours, nobody can say. But to sacrifice a hair of the head of your vision, a shade of its colour, in deference to some Headmaster with a silver pot in his hand or to some professor with a measuring-rod up his sleeve, is the most abject treachery, and the sacrifice of wealth and chastity which used to be said to be the greatest of human disasters, a mere flea-bite in comparison.

Next I think that you may object that in all this I have made too much of the importance of material things. Even allowing a generous margin for symbolism, that five hundred a year stands for the power to contemplate, that a lock on the door means the power to think for oneself, still you may say that the mind should rise above such things; and that great poets have often been poor men. Let me then quote to you the words of your own Professor of Literature, who knows better than I do what goes to the making of a poet. Sir Arthur Quiller-Couch writes:[1]

"What are the great poetical names of the last hundred years or so? Coleridge, Wordsworth, Byron, Shelley, Landor, Keats, Tennyson, Browning, Arnold, Morris, Rossetti, Swinburne—we may stop there. Of these, all but Keats, Browning, Rossetti were University men; and of these three, Keats, who died young, cut off in his prime, was the only one not fairly well to do. It may seem a brutal thing to say, and it is a sad thing to say: but, as a matter of hard fact, the theory that poetical genius

[1] *The Art of Writing,* by Sir Arthur Quiller-Couch.

bloweth where it listeth, and equally in poor and rich, holds little truth. As a matter of hard fact, nine out of those twelve were University men: which means that somehow or other they procured the means to get the best education England can give. As a matter of hard fact, of the remaining three you know that Browning was well to do, and I challenge you that, if he had not been well to do, he would no more have attained to write *Saul* or *The Ring and the Book* than Ruskin would have attained to writing *Modern Painters* if his father had not dealt prosperously in business. Rossetti had a small private income; and, moreover, he painted. There remains but Keats; whom Atropos slew young, as she slew John Clare in a mad-house, and James Thomson by the laudanum he took to drug disappointment. These are dreadful facts but let us face them. It is—however dishonouring to us as a nation—certain that, by some fault in our commonwealth, the poor poet has not in these days, nor has had for two hundred years, a dog's chance. Believe me—and I have spent a great part of ten years in watching some three hundred and twenty elementary schools—we may prate of democracy, but actually, a poor child in England has little more hope than had the son of an Athenian slave to be emancipated into that intellectual freedom of which great writings are born."

Nobody could put the point more plainly. "The poor poet has not in these days, nor has had for two hundred years, a dog's chance . . . a poor child in England has little more hope than had the son of an Athenian slave to be emancipated into that intellectual freedom of which great writings are born." That is it. Intellectual freedom depends upon material things. Poetry depends upon intellectual freedom. And women have always been poor, not for two hundred years merely, but from the beginning of time. Women have had less intellectual freedom than the sons of Athenian slaves. Women, then, have not had a dog's chance of writing poetry. That is why I have laid so much stress on money and a room of one's own. However, thanks to the toils of those obscure women in the past, of whom I wish we knew more, thanks, curiously enough, to two wars, the Crimean which let Florence Nightingale out of her drawing-room, and the European War which opened the doors to the average woman some sixty years later, these evils are in the way to be bettered. Otherwise you would not be here tonight, and your chance of earning five hundred pounds a year, precarious as I am afraid that it still is, would be minute in the extreme.

Still, you may object, why do you attach so much importance to this writing of books by women when, according to you, it requires so much effort, leads perhaps to the murder of one's aunts, will make one almost certainly late for luncheon, and may bring one into very grave disputes with certain very good fellows? My motives, let me admit, are partly selfish. Like most uneducated Englishwomen, I like reading—I like reading books in the bulk. Lately my diet has become a trifle monotonous; history is too much about wars; biography too much about great men; poetry has shown, I think, a tendency to sterility, and fiction—but I have sufficiently exposed my disabilities as a critic of modern fiction and will say no more about it. Therefore I would ask you to write all kinds of books, hesitating at no subject however trivial or however vast. By hook or by crook, I hope that you will possess yourselves of money enough to travel and to idle, to contemplate the future or the past of the world, to dream over books and loiter at street corners and let the line of thought dip deep into the stream. For I am by no means confining you to fiction. If you would please me—and there are thousands like me—you would write books of travel and adventure, and research and scholarship, and history and biography, and criticism and philosophy and science. By so doing you will certainly profit the art of fiction. For books have a way of influencing each other. Fiction will be much the better for standing cheek by jowl with poetry and philosophy. Moreover, if you consider any great figure of the past, like Sappho, like the Lady Murasaki, like Emily Brontë, you will find that she is an inheritor as well as an originator, and has come into existence because women have come to have the habit of writing naturally; so that even as a prelude to poetry such activity on your part would be invaluable.

But when I look back through these notes and criticise my own train of thought as I made them, I find that my motives were not altogether selfish. There runs through these comments and discursions the conviction—or is it the instinct?—that good books are desirable and that good writers, even if they show every variety of human depravity, are still good human beings. Thus when I ask you to write more books I am urging you to do what will be for your good and for the good of the world at large. How to justify this instinct or belief I do not know, for philosophic words, if one has not been educated at a university, are apt to play one false. What is meant by "reality"? It would seem to be something very erratic, very undependable—now to be found in a dusty road, now in a scrap of newspaper in the street, now in a daffodil in the sun. It lights up a group in a room and stamps some casual saying. It overwhelms one walking home beneath the stars and makes the silent world more real than the world of speech—and then there it is again in an omnibus in the uproar of Piccadilly. Sometimes, too, it seems to dwell in shapes too far away for us to discern what their nature is. But whatever it touches, it fixes and makes permanent. That is what remains over when the skin of the day has been cast into the hedge; that is what is left of past time and of our loves and hates. Now the writer, as I think, has the chance to live more than other people in the presence of this reality. It is his business to find it and collect it and communicate it to the rest of us. So at least I infer from reading *Lear* or *Emma* or *La Recherche du Temps Perdu*. For the reading of these books seems to perform a curious couching operation on the senses; one sees more intensely afterwards; the world seems bared of its covering and given an intenser life. Those are the enviable people who live at enmity with unreality; and those are the pitiable who are knocked on the head by the thing done without knowing or caring. So that when I ask you to earn money and have a room of your own, I am asking you to live in the presence of reality, an invigorating life, it would appear, whether one can impart it or not.

Here I would stop, but the pressure of convention decrees that every speech must end with a peroration. And a peroration addressed to women should have something, you will agree, particularly exalting and ennobling about it. I should implore you to remember your responsibilities, to be higher, more spiritual; I should remind you how much depends upon you, and what an influence you can exert upon the future. But those exhortations can safely, I think, be left to the other sex, who will put them, and indeed have put them, with far greater eloquence than I can compass. When I rummage in my own mind I find no noble sentiments about being companions and equals and influencing the world to higher ends. I find myself saying briefly and prosaically that it is much more important to be oneself than anything else. Do not dream of influencing other people, I would say, if I knew how to make it sound exalted. Think of things in themselves.

And again I am reminded by dipping into newspapers and novels and biographies that when a woman speaks to women she should have something very unpleasant up her sleeve. Women are hard on women. Women dislike women. Women— but are you not sick to death of the word? I can assure you that I am. Let us agree, then, that a paper read by a woman to women should end with something particularly disagreeable.

But how does it go? What can I think of? The truth is, I often like women. I like their unconventionality. I like their subtlety. I like their anonymity. I like—but I must not run on in this way. That cupboard there,—you say it holds clean table-napkins only; but what if Sir Archibald Bodkin were concealed among them? Let me then adopt a sterner tone. Have I, in the preceding words, conveyed to you sufficiently the warnings and reprobation of mankind? I have told you the very low opinion in which you were held by Mr. Oscar Browning. I have indicated what Napoleon once thought of you and what Mussolini thinks now. Then, in case any of you aspire to fiction, I have copied out for your benefit the advice of the critic about courageously acknowledging the limitations of your sex. I have referred to Professor X and given prominence to his statement that women are intellectually, morally and physically inferior to men. I have handed on all that has come my way without going in search of it, and here is a final warning—from Mr. John Langdon Davies.[2] Mr. John Langdon Davies warns women "that when children cease to be altogether desirable, women cease to be altogether necessary." I hope you will make a note of it.

How can I further encourage you to go about the business of life? Young women, I would say, and please attend, for the peroration is beginning, you are, in my opinion, disgracefully ignorant. You have never made a discovery of any sort of importance. You have never shaken an empire or led an army into battle. The plays of Shakespeare are not by you, and you have never introduced a barbarous race to the blessings of civilisation. What is your excuse? It is all very well for you to say, pointing to the streets and squares and forests of the globe swarming with black and white and coffee-coloured inhabitants, all busily engaged in traffic and enterprise and love-making, we have had other work on our hands. Without our doing, those seas would be unsailed and those fertile lands a desert. We have borne and

[2]*A Short History of Women*, by John Langdon Davies.

bred and washed and taught, perhaps to the age of six or seven years, the one thousand six hundred and twenty-three million human beings who are, according to statistics, at present in existence, and that, allowing that some had help, takes time.

There is truth in what you say—I will not deny it. But at the same time may I remind you that there have been at least two colleges for women in existence in England since the year 1866; that after the year 1880 a married woman was allowed by law to possess her own property; and that in 1919—which is a whole nine years ago—she was given a vote? May I also remind you that most of the professions have been open to you for close on ten years now? When you reflect upon these immense privileges and the length of time during which they have been enjoyed, and the fact that there must be at this moment some two thousand women capable of earning over five hundred a year in one way or another, you will agree that the excuse of lack of opportunity, training, encouragement, leisure and money no longer holds good. Moreover, the economists are telling us that Mrs. Seton has had too many children. You must, of course, go on bearing children, but, so they say, in twos and threes, not in tens and twelves.

Thus, with some time on your hands and with some book learning in your brains—you have had enough of the other kind, and are sent to college partly, I suspect, to be uneducated—surely you should embark upon another stage of your very long, very laborious and highly obscure career. A thousand pens are ready to suggest what you should do and what effect you will have. My own suggestion is a little fantastic, I admit; I prefer, therefore, to put it in the form of fiction.

I told you in the course of this paper that Shakespeare had a sister; but do not look for her in Sir Sidney Lee's life of the poet. She died young—alas, she never wrote a word. She lies buried where the omnibuses now stop, opposite the Elephant and Castle. Now my belief is that this poet who never wrote a word and was buried at the crossroads still lives. She lives in you and in me, and in many other women who are not here tonight, for they are washing up the dishes and putting the children to bed. But she lives; for great poets do not die; they are continuing presences; they need only the opportunity to walk among us in the flesh. This opportunity, as I think, it is now coming within your power to give her. For my belief is that if we live another century or so—I am talking of the common life which is the real life and not of the little separate lives which we live as individuals—and have five hundred a year each of us and rooms of our own; if we have the habit of freedom and the courage to write exactly what we think; if we escape a little from the common sitting-room and see human beings not always in their relation to each other but in relation to reality; and the sky, too, and the trees or whatever it may be in themselves; if we look past Milton's bogey, for no human being should shut out the view; if we face the fact, for it is a fact, that there is no arm to cling to, but that we go alone and that our relation is to the world of reality and not only to the world of men and women, then the opportunity will come and the dead poet who was Shakespeare's sister will put on the body which she has so often laid down. Drawing her life from the lives of the unknown who were her forerunners, as her brother did before her, she will be born. As for her coming without that preparation, without that effort on our part, without that determination that when she is born again she shall find it possible to live and write her poetry, that we cannot expect, for that would be impossible. But I maintain that she would come if we worked for her, and that so to work, even in poverty and obscurity, is worth while.

Arts Society . . . Odtaa [3n]   Newnham, founded in 1871, and Girton, founded in 1869, were colleges for women at Cambridge University, which did not at that time award degrees to women. The Girton society took its name from a novel by John Masefield entitled *Odtaa* (1926), an acronym meaning "one damn thing after another."

Chapter One

a few remarks about [3]   British writers Frances Burney (1752–1840); Jane Austen (1775–1817); Charlotte Brontë (1816–1855), Emily Brontë (1818–1848), Anne Brontë (1820–1849), who lived in their father's Yorkshire parsonage in Haworth; Mary Russell Mitford (1787–1855); George Eliot, the pseudonym for Marian Evans (1819–1880); and Elizabeth Gaskell (1810–1865). Mitford was known for her sketches and verse about rural life, the others for their celebrated novels.

Oxbridge [4]   A frequently used term conflating Oxford and Cambridge.

Fernham [4]   Based upon Newnham and Girton, the two women's colleges at Cambridge, but with a consonant change that brings to mind ferns. In a struck-out typescript version, Fernham is called St. Miriams (Rosenbaum 180).

Mary Beton, Mary Seton, Mary Carmichael [5]   The "Ballad of the
Four Marys," also sometimes called "Ballad of Mary Hamilton,"
has a refrain: "Yesterday the queen had four Marys; / This night
she'll have but three; / There was Mary Beaton and Mary
Seaton / Mary Carmichael and me." The "me" is Mary Hamilton, a lady-in-waiting about to be hanged (sometimes by the
queen) because of an illicit sexual relationship and resulting
pregnancy (sometimes by the king) as well as, in some versions,
an infanticide. Assumed to refer to the sixteenth-century court
of Mary, Queen of Scots, or to the eighteenth-century court of
Russia's Czar Peter. The names of the ballad recur as subsequent
characters in Woolf's text. The American version reprinted
below comes from a Joan Baez songbook:

Word is to the kitchen gone
And word is to the hall,
And word is up to Madame the Queen
And that's the worst of all,
That Mary Hamilton's borne a babe to the highest Stuart of all.

"Arise, arise, Mary Hamilton,
Arise and tell to me,
What thou hast done with thy wee babe
I saw and heard weep by thee?"

"I put him in a tiny boat,
And cast him out to sea,
That he might sink or he might swim,
But he'd never come back to me."

"Arise, arise, Mary Hamilton,
Arise and come with me;
There is a wedding in Glasgow town,
This night we'll go and see."

She put not on her robes of black,
Nor her robes of brown,
But she put on her robes of white,
To ride into Glasgow town.

And as she rode into Glasgow town,
The city for to see,
The bailiff's wife and the provost's wife
Cried, "Ach, and alas for thee."

"Ah, you need not weep for me," she cried,
"You need not weep for me;
For had I not slain my own wee babe,
This death I would not dee."

"Ah, little did my mother think
When first she cradled me,
The lands I was to travel in,
And the death I was to dee."

"Last night I washed the Queen's feet,
And put the gold on her hair,
And the only reward I find for this,
The gallows to be my share."

"Cast off, cast off my gown," she cried,
"But let my petticoat be,
And tie a napkin 'round my face;
The gallows I would not see."

Then by and come the King himself,
Looked up with a pitiful eye,
"Come down, come down, Mary Hamilton,
Tonight you'll dine with me."

"Ah, hold your tongue, my sovereign liege,
And let your folly be;
For if you'd a mind to save my life
You'd never have shamed me here."

"Last night there were four Marys,
Tonight there'll be but three,
There was Mary Beaton, and Mary Seaton,
And Mary Carmichael and me."

Many variants can be found in *The English and Scottish Popular Ballads,* edited by F. J. Child (1825–1896); the five opening stanzas of one version, from *Sharpe's Ballad Book of 1824,* are reprinted below:

Word's gane to the kitchen,
    And word's gane to the ha,
That Marie Hamilton gangs wi bairn
    To the hichest Stewart of a'.

He's courted her in the kitchen,
    He's courted her in the ha,
He's courted her in the laigh cellar,
    And that was warst of a'.

She's tied it in her apron
    And she's thrown it in the sea;
Says, Sink ye, swim ye, bonny wee babe!
    You'l never get mair of me.

Down then came the auld queen,
    Gold tassels tying her hair:
'O Marie, where's the bonny wee babe
    That I heard greet sae sair?'

> 'There never was a babe intill my room,
>   As little designs to be;
> It was but a touch o my sair side,
>   Come oer my fair bodie.'

a Beadle [6]   A university official, historically associated with a minor parish officer in the Church of England who kept order in church.

Fellows and Scholars [6]   According to the *Oxford English Dictionary*, terms (corresponding to the Latin *socius*) given to the incorporated members of a college or collegiate foundation. The fellows were often included under the term *scholar*. The latter term is, in later use, mostly restricted to junior members of the foundation, who are still under tuition; the term *fellow* is applied to senior scholars, who have graduated or passed out of the state of tutelage.

Charles Lamb . . . Thackeray [6]   English essayist (1775–1834), whose "Oxford in the Vacation" (1820) describes his shock at seeing the "original written copy" of "Lycidas": "How it staggered me to see the fine things in their ore! interlined, corrected! as if their words were mortal, alterable, displacable at pleasure!" See *The Works of Charles and Mary Lamb*, edited by E. V. Lucas, vol. II, 1903. William Makepeace Thackeray (1811–1863) was a prominent Victorian novelist. Woolf's father was married to Thackeray's daughter Harriet until her death in 1875.

Max Beerbohm [7]   English satirist (1872–1956) who corresponded with Woolf and whose comic heroine in *Zuleika Dobson* (1911) arrives to triumph at Oxford, where the busts of Roman emperors weep.

Lycidas [7]   Arguably the most famous English pastoral elegy (1638), written by John Milton (1608–1674). The poem mourns the death of his friend from Cambridge, Edward King, and its manuscript is housed in the Wren Library at Trinity College, Cambridge.

Thackeray's Esmond [7]   *The History of Henry Esmond, Esquire* (1852) by William Makepeace Thackeray was composed in the style of an eighteenth-century fiction.

the Strand [9]   A busy street in London, running from Fleet Street to Trafalgar Square and through some of the busiest business districts in London.

at the sound of a whistle [9]   "Five versions appear in the manuscript ["Women & Fiction"] of the joke about the professor who is said to gallop if someone whistles," according to Rosenbaum (xxiv).

these stones on a deep foundation [9]   King's College Chapel, Cambridge, was built from 1446 to 1547.

luncheon [10]   An imaginative rendering of a lunch at King's College, in George Rylands's rooms on October 21, 1928, the day after the first lecture version of *A Room* was delivered. A member of the so-called Cambridge Apostles, Rylands (1902–1999) briefly worked for the Woolfs at the Hogarth Press in 1924; his dissertation and verse were subsequently published by the Press.

We are all going to heaven [11]   These are the reputed last words of Thomas Gainsborough (1727–1788), English painter of portraits and landscapes. They refer to the Antwerp-born Sir Anthony Van Dyck (1599–1641), who painted portraits of the English royal family.

Manx cat [11]   In "Women & Fiction," the cat without a tail brings to mind unspecified thoughts which the narrator leaves "to Freud" to explain (Rosenbaum 14). In 1920 Woolf reviewed Aldous Huxley's *Limbo,* which also contains an allusion to a Manx cat.

before the war [11]   Unprecedented (as its name suggests), World War I (1914–1918) destroyed an entire generation of young men in battles with casualties that far exceeded those of any other war before or after. A watershed in modernism, it ushered in an age of disillusionment among the members of the so-called lost generation, many of whom became convinced that traditional beliefs and values had been annihilated.

There has fallen [12]   From the long poem *Maud* (1855), part 1, section 22, stanza 10, composed by Alfred, Lord Tennyson (1809–1892), Victorian poet laureate, and focused on violence, family discord, madness. Its speaker, a man depressed after his father's suicide, is restored by the love of Maud. Although he eventually loses her, he finds resolution by enlisting to fight in the Crimean War. Tennyson is satirized in Woolf's farce *Freshwater*.

My heart is like [12]   From "A Birthday" (1861) by Christina Rossetti (1830–1894), the subject of Woolf's essay "'I am Christina Rossetti.'" After the first stanza quoted by Woolf, another stanza closes the poem (which is partly cited in the draft version "Women & Fiction"):

> Raise me a dais of silk and down;
>   Hang it with vair and purple dyes;
> Carve it in doves and pomegranates,
>   And peacocks with a hundred eyes;
> Work it in gold and silver grapes,
>   In leaves and silver fleurs-de-lys;
> Because the birthday of my life
>   Is come, my love is come to me.

Isle of Man [13]   Two hundred twenty-seven square miles, an island in the Irish Sea, some sixty miles west of the Lancashire coast. Supposedly the place of origin of the Manx cat, sometimes referred to as the "Dog Cat."

a road—I forget its name [13]   Cambridge's colleges for women, which were established in the late nineteenth century, are outside the much older university area.

towards Headingley [14]   An Oxford suburb called Headington and a Headington road connecting it to Oxford may have been misremembered or deliberately changed by Woolf, according to Benjamin Harvey.

J—H— [17]   Jane Harrison (1850–1928), a scholar in classical archaeology who was also interested in psychology and in the female divinities within ancient Greek religions. A fellow at Newnham College, she authored many influential books, including *Ancient Art and Ritual* (1913). Her *Reminiscences of a Student's Life* was published by the Hogarth Press in 1925. Woolf's *Diary* records her 1928 visit to Harrison on her deathbed (3: 180). Given Harrison's death date, she is "an anachronistic fantasy" and in *Women & Fiction* only one of several dead academic figures mentioned: "Mr Verrall? Mr Sidgwick? Jane Harrison?" (Rosenbaum xxiv and 23).

in Trinity or Somerville . . . or Christchurch [18]   Trinity is a college of Cambridge, while Somerville and Christchurch are at Oxford.

Mary Seton [18]   An allusion to the Child ballad. Mary Seton in the draft eventually moves to Australia, where she keeps a horse and ostriches (Rosenbaum 26–27).

head of the dead king . . . at Windsor [19]   In 1813, as a consequence of excavations in St. George's Chapel of Windsor, the vault containing King Charles I was found by workmen. When the coffin was opened and the cloth around the body unwrapped, according to an eyewitness, " 'the left eye, in the first moment of exposure was full and open, but vanished almost immediately'" (Charles Wheeler Coit, *The Royal Martyr* [London: Selwyn and Blount, 1924]).

what John Stuart Mill said [20]   English philosopher (1806–1873) whose *The Subjection of Women* (1869) argued for women's right to equality.

Monte Carlo [21]   A gambling resort in Monaco.

the Parthenon [21]   Doric temple of Athena, built on the Acropolis in Athens and often visited by tourists in Greece.

only for the last forty-eight years [22]   In 1870 the Married Women's Property Act allowed married women to retain £200 of their own earnings (which previously became the property of their husbands); in 1884 another act gave married women the same property rights as unmarried women, allowing both to carry on trades or businesses using their property.

Balliol or Kings [23]   Colleges at Oxford and Cambridge.

at St. Andrews [23]   St. Andrew Holborn, a church in London designed by Sir Christopher Wren (1632–1723).

tufts of fur [24]   The Cambridge academic hood is fringed with rabbit fur.

not a boots [24]   "A name for the servant in hotels who cleans the boots; formerly called *boot-catch* and *–catch*" (*Oxford English Dictionary*).

Chapter Two

British Museum [25]   Woolf studies inside the famous reading room in Bloomsbury. In *Women & Fiction,* a passage struck out takes up a point Woolf had considered in *Jacob's Room:* "Yet only the

~~names of men encircle the proud dome of the British Museum Reading room~~" (Rosenbaum 49).

Lord Birkenhead's opinion of [29]   An opponent of women's suffrage, F. E. Smith, Earl of Birkenhead (1872–1930), was lord chancellor from 1919 to 1922.

Dean Inge's opinion of [29]   William Ralph Inge (1860–1954), dean of St. Paul's Cathedral in London from 1911 to 1934.

Dr. Johnson's opinion of [29]   The prominent critic and literary man Samuel Johnson (1709–1784) is quoted below.

Mr. Oscar Browning's opinion of [29]   A history lecturer at King's College, Cambridge, Oscar Browning (1837–1923) reappears in the third chapter.

Samuel Butler [29]   A British satirist and novelist (1835–1902), he published *The Authoress of the Odyssey* in 1897 and *The Way of All Flesh* in 1903.

Pope [29]   Satirized in *Orlando,* Alexander Pope (1688–1744) was a verse satirist, and the line quoted here comes from one of his "Moral Essays," "Of the Characters of Women" (1735). It appears at the very start of the poem: "Nothing so true as what you once let fall, / *Most Women have no Characters at all.*" The work ends by praising woman as "a *softer Man.*"

La Bruyère [29]   Jean de La Bruyère (1645–1696) was a French moralist; in translation, the quotation from *The Characters: Women* means "Women are extreme; they are better or worse than men."

Napoleon [30]   Napoléon Bonaparte (1769–1821) became the emperor of France in 1804.

"Men know..." [30n]   Woolf here quotes James Boswell (1740–1795), whose *Life of Samuel Johnson* appeared in 1791.

half divine and worship them [30n]   British anthropologist James Frazer (1854–1941) published his immensely influential study of ancient and primitive myth, magic, ritual, and taboo in twelve volumes (1911–15) that were eventually abridged in 1922.

Goethe [30]   Johann Wolfgang von Goethe was a prominent German poet, novelist, and playwright (1749–1832). The first part of his *Faust* (1808) features an innocent heroine, Margaret, condemned to death for murdering her illegitimate child by Faust.

Mussolini [30]   The Italian Fascist dictator known as *Il Duce,* Benito Mussolini (1883–1945) formed an alliance with Nazi Germany during World War II and contributed to the Fascist cult of maternity for the "fatherland."

Professor von X. [31]   In *Women & Fiction,* his prototype, Professor X, appears arguing "~~(at a table in a bier halle)~~" (45), and angered either by his wife's disparaging remarks about his looks or about not getting a university appointment. The German "von" does not appear in the draft. Some scholars consider his book a reference to Otto Weininger's *Sex and Character* (1903), an influential treatise on bisexuality that has been criticized for its misogyny and anti-Semitism.

astrachan [31]   Probably meaning astrakhan, which is the silk of young lambs from Russia; the wool resembles fur and is used for edging garments.

Freudian theory [31]   By the time of *A Room*'s composition, Woolf was familiar with the psychoanalytic writings of Sigmund Freud (1856–1939), whose translated works she and her husband would publish at the Hogarth Press. In 1939, on the one occasion when the exiled, dying Freud met Woolf and they discussed their common horror at the rise of Hitler, he handed her a narcissus.

ready-made tie [32]   A deprecatory allusion to the inferiority of clothing not made to order and thus presumably an indication of the student's class.

faggot burning on the top of Hampstead Heath [32]   A bundle of sticks set ablaze on an open area of land in a suburb of London where Woolf lived for some time. The phrase might call to mind either Moses's burning bush or the bonfires built on Guy Fawkes Day (November 5), when Britain's most famous conspirator (against James I) is burned in effigy.

Sir Austen Chamberlain [33]   The foreign secretary at the time of *A Room*'s composition, Chamberlain (1863–1937) was brother of Neville Chamberlain (1869–1940), British prime minister (1937–40) at the start of World War II.

portrait of a grandfather by Romney [35]   George Romney (1734–1802) was a fashionable portrait painter.

some book by Rebecca West [35]   Cicily Isabel Fairfield (1892–1983) took her pen name from Ibsen's play *Rosmersholm* (1886) about a radical feminist named Rebecca West. She argued for free love and women's trade unions, and against conservative divorce laws in radical journalism preceding the First World War; and later produced a number of novels, biographical studies, and travel books.

The Czar and the Kaiser [35]   Dictators of Russia and Germany, respectively.

Napoleon and Mussolini [35]   Mentioned earlier in terms of their derogation of women.

five hundred pounds a year for ever [37]   An equivalent inheritance today would consist of approximately $37,000 a year.

before 1918 [37]   A date that could refer either to the granting of women's suffrage to those thirty years of age or the pre–World War I period. Women twenty-one years of age and older were given the vote in 1928.

one gift . . . to hide [37]   John Milton's sonnet "On His Blindness" begins "When I consider how my light is spent, / E'er half my days, in this dark world and wide, / And that one Talent which is death to hide, / Lodg'd with me useless, though my soul more bent / To serve therewith my Maker."

harbouring . . . an eagle, a vulture [38]   A conflation of the mythic punishment of Prometheus and the story of the Spartan boy who stole a fox and let it tear his chest and kill him rather than betray his theft.

Admiralty Arch [38]   Constructed from 1906 to 1911 to commemorate Britain's imperial successes, it stands between the Mall and Trafalgar Square in London.

the statue of the Duke of Cambridge [38]   Unveiled in 1907 to honor the Duke (1819–1904) who had served as commander in chief of the British Army, the statue was designed by Adrian Jones and stands in front of the War Offices, down Whitehall from the Admiralty Arch.

a gentleman, which Milton recommended [39]   One of several allusions to John Milton, the "gentleman" might be a mocking reference to God, Adam, an ordained minister, or the poet himself.

saw an aeroplane [40]   Airplanes played a quite minor role in World War I, though by the late twenties technology was beginning to turn them into the powerful weaponry they would constitute in the Second World War. Possibly also a reference back to the skywriting airplane in *Mrs. Dalloway*.

Chapter Three

time of Elizabeth [41]   Depicted in *Orlando,* Elizabeth Tudor (1533–1603) ascended the throne in 1558. Her reign is associated with the prolific literary age called the Renaissance and specifically with the plays of William Shakespeare.

Professor Trevelyan's History of England [42]   G. M. Trevelyan's (1876–1962) *History of England* (1926) was a standard one-volume history of the country; he was a professor at Cambridge.

Chaucer's time [42]   Geoffrey Chaucer (c. 1340–1400) was the author of *The Canterbury Tales.*

time of the Stuarts [42]   The Stuart monarchs reigned from 1603 to 1714, or from James I to Anne. The Stuart line ended because none of Anne's eighteen children survived to adulthood.

like the Verneys and the Hutchinsons [42]   Both family histories were penned by women. Frances Parthenope, Lady Verney edited *Memoirs of the Verney Family during the Seventeenth Century* (1925), and Lucy Hutchinson wrote *Memoirs of the Life of Colonel Hutchinson ... to which is Prefixed the Life of Mrs. Hutchinson, Written by Herself* (1810).

Cleopatra ... Lady Macbeth ... Rosalind [42]   Commanding female characters in the plays of Shakespeare, specifically the queen of Egypt in *Antony and Cleopatra,* the ambitious wife in *Macbeth,* and the cross-dresser in *As You Like It.*

Clytemnestra, Antigone, ... Phèdre, Cressida, ... Desdemona, the Duchess of Malfi [42–43]   Doomed but powerful heroines in Aeschylus's *Agamemnon,* Sophocles' *Antigone,* Shakespeare's *Troilus and Cressida,* Shakespeare's *Othello,* and Webster's *The Duchess of Malfi.*

Millamant, Clarissa, Becky Sharp, Anna Karenina, Emma Bovary, Madame de Guermantes [43]   Heroines famed for their wit, beauty, or imaginative powers from seventeenth-, eighteenth-, and nineteenth-century literature, in William Congreve's *The Way of the World*, Samuel Richardson's *Clarissa*, Thackeray's *Vanity Fair*, Leo Tolstoy's *Anna Karenina*, Gustav Flaubert's *Madame Bovary*, and, from the twentieth century, Marcel Proust's multivolume *Remembrance of Things Past*.

odalisque [43n]   A concubine in a harem.

Cassandra... [43n]   Lucas discusses heroines in *Agamemnon* and *The Persians* by Aeschylus and Euripides' *Medea*.

Hermione... [43n]   Passionate and headstrong heroines of *Andromaque* (1667), *Bérénice* (1670), *Bajazet* (1772), *Phèdre* (1677), and *Athalie* (1691) by French playwright Jean Racine (1639–1699).

Solveig... [43n]   Intelligent and mindful women featured in Henrik Ibsen's (1828–1906) *Peer Gynt* (1867), *A Doll's House* (1879), *Hedda Gabler* (1890), *The Master Builder* (1892), and *Rosmersholm* (1886). The last character in this list inspired the pseudonym of novelist Rebecca West (1892–1983).

the property of her husband [43]   As *femes [sic] covert*, married women had practically no legal rights; they were "covered" or legally represented by their husbands.

Aubrey hardly mentions her [44]   John Aubrey (1626–1697) collected anecdotes and gossip in his diaries.

Joanna Baillie... the poetry of Edgar Allan Poe [45]   A Scots poet and dramatist, Joanna Baillie (1762–1851) published during the Romantic period; the American short story writer and poet Edgar Allan Poe (1809–1849) was well-known for tales of horror and ballads.

homes and haunts of... Mitford [45]   Mentioned at the beginning of *A Room*, Mary Russell Mitford (1787–1855) was known for her writing about rural life.

a wonderfully gifted sister, called Judith [46]   William Shakespeare did
have a daughter named Judith Quinney Shakespeare (1585–1662),
the twin of Hamnet. In the draft "Women & Fiction," Judith
Shakespeare is named Mary Arden, after William Shakespeare's
mother. Her father is described as a tradesman or butcher, her
mother an heiress or of gentle birth (Rosenbaum 73). She is also
said to have once gone "gallivanting off in the woods dressed like
a man" (74). Tillie Olsen and Jane Marcus have linked Judith
Shakespeare to William Black's historical novel *Judith Shakespeare*
(1883) and to a passage in Olive Schreiner's *From Man to Man*
(1926), in which the question is posed, "what of the possible
Shakespeares we might have had, who passed their life from
youth upward brewing currant wine and making pastries for fat
country squires to eat. ..." (p. 195). Woolf's "The Mark on the
Wall" and *Orlando* present other portraits of William Shakespeare.

Ovid, Virgil and Horace [46]   Three Roman poets of the Augustan
period (27 B.C.–A.D. 14) whose works were part of a standard
training in the classics for English schoolboys.

a neighbouring wool-stapler [47]   A dealer in the staple of wool.

poodles dancing and women acting [47]   An allusion to Samuel Johnson's belief that "a woman's preaching is like a dog's walking on
his hinder legs. It is not done well; but you are surprised to find
it done at all" (Boswell, *Life of Samuel Johnson*, 31 July 1763). During the Renaissance, women's roles were generally played by
male actors, often by boys.

Nick Greene [48]   In *Orlando* (1928), Nick Greene is first a creative
writer, later a severe literary critic who survives from the Renaissance until modern times. One Robert Greene (1558–1592)
published pamphlets and dramas in the Elizabethan period, including an early derogatory reference to Shakespeare in his
Greene's Groatsworth of Wit (1592).

Elephant and Castle [48]   A famous tavern south of the Thames (on the outskirts of London) and at a busy crossroads; also a major tube stop on the Bakerloo line that first opened in 1906. Suicides were traditionally buried at a crossroads to prevent their spirits from returning.

Emily Brontë or a Robert Burns [48]   The famed author of *Wuthering Heights* (1847) and the famed author (1759–1796) of Scots ballads, often written in dialect.

mute and inglorious Jane Austen [48]   An echo of Thomas Gray's *Elegy Written in a Country Churchyard* (1751), line 59: "Some mute inglorious Milton here may rest."

Edward Fitzgerald [49]   English scholar and poet (1809–1883) who translated *The Rubáiyát of Omar Khayyám.*

Currer Bell . . . name of a man [50]   In this discussion of the male pseudonym, Currer Bell is the name Charlotte Brontë used at the start of her career; George Eliot was the name adopted by Marian Evans throughout her publishing history; George Sand, the pseudonym of Amandine-Aurore-Lucie Dupin. All were nineteenth-century novelists of renown.

Pericles [50]   Athenian statesman and orator (c. 495–429 B.C.).

Ce chien est à moi [50]   This dog is mine (French), from Blaise Pascal's *Pensées*, 64. Naomi Black has pointed out that this phrase served as an epigraph to Leonard Woolf's anti-imperialist *Empire and Commerce in Africa.*

Parliament Square, the Sièges Allée [50]   London site for memorial statues; a busy thoroughfare in Berlin, Avenue of Victory.

a very fine negress [50]   Taken by a number of contemporary critics to signal Woolf's fetishizing of the black woman here (and by Jaime Hovey in *Orlando*).

"never blotted a line" [51]   In *Timber*, Ben Jonson recalled actors having "mentioned it as an honour to Shakespeare that in his writing (whatsoever he penned) he never blotted out a line."

Rousseau [51]   Jean-Jacques Rousseau (1712–1778) was a French philosopher and writer who published his *Confessions* (1782–89).

Carlyle . . . Flaubert . . . Keats [51]   Thomas Carlyle (1795–1881), Scots philosopher and historian whose *French Revolution* appeared in 1837. Gustave Flaubert (1821–1880), French novelist whose *Madame Bovary* was published in 1857; John Keats (1795–1821), British Romantic poet whose letters describe the difficulties he faced as a writer.

"Mighty poets in their misery dead" [51]   From William Wordsworth's *Resolution and Independence* (1807), line 116. The line refers to Chatterton and Burns, both of whom came to "despondency and madness," according to Wordsworth.

pin money [52]   The allowance husbands gave their wives for personal needs. The expression derives from Catherine Howard, wife of Henry VIII, who introduced pins into England from France; because they were expensive, a separate sum for this luxury was granted ladies by their husbands.

Lord Birkenhead [52]   Mentioned at the beginning of the second chapter, Frederick Edwin Smith, Lord Birkenhead (1872–1930), was a Conservative politician and lord chancellor at the time of *A Room*'s composition.

Dean Inge [52]   Mentioned earlier, Inge (1860–1954) was the dean of St. Paul's Cathedral in London.

Harley Street specialist [52]   Many prestigious medical specialists have offices on London's Harley Street, including Woolf's fictional Dr. Bradshaw in *Mrs. Dalloway*.

Mr. Oscar Browning [53]   A Fellow of King's College, Cambridge, Oscar Browning recorded his life in *Memories of Sixty Years* (1910). Woolf's source was a biography his nephew H. E. Wortham published in 1927. Jane Marcus argues that this biography revealed to Woolf the misogyny of the men in her own family.

Mr. Greg [53]   The English essayist William Rathbone Greg (1809–1891) whose 1862 essay "Why Are Women Redundant?" is misquoted by Woolf: His "they" refers specifically to female servants. The quote reads: "In a word, they [servants] fulfill both essentials of a woman's being; they are supported by, and they minister to, men. We could not possibly do without them." For this reason, Greg does not include single female servants in his category of "redundant" women.

Germaine Tailleferre [54]   A French composer (1892–1983), she was the only female member of the Groupe des Six in Paris during the twenties, and a friend of Stravinsky, Diaghilev, Ravel, and Picasso.

Lady Bessborough . . . to Lord Granville Leveson-Gower [54–55]   Lady Bessborough is Henrietta, countess of Bessborough (1761–1821); the private correspondence of Leveson-Gower (1773–1846) was published in 1916, edited by Castalia, Countess Granville.

cock-a-doodle-dum [55]   In *Women & Fiction,* there is a more extended analysis of "this Cock-a-doodling" (162) of male authors.

Florence Nightingale [55]   The famous pioneer in nursing (1820–1910) grappled with issues of self-definition in 1851 and 1852, but *Cassandra* was not publicly printed until 1928, when Ray Strachey included it in her history of the women's movement. Many more sentences in the manuscript are devoted to the effect of the

Crimean War and Florence Nightingale on women's history (see, for example, Rosenbaum 183–84).

words he had cut [55]   Keats's tombstone reads, "Here lies one whose name was writ in water."

Chapter Four

Lady Winchilsea [57]   Anne Finch, Countess of Winchilsea (1661–1720), published one collection of verse in her lifetime, in 1713.

How are we fallen! [58]   The passage quoted is from Anne Finch's "The Introduction" (1713), lines 51–58.

Alas! a woman [58]   From Anne Finch's "The Introduction," lines 9–20.

To some few [59]   The last three lines of Finch's "The Introduction."

Nor will in fading [59]   From Anne Finch, "The Spleen" (1713), a poem on the "humor" or personality feature thought to cause depression or melancholy, lines 85–86.

Mr. Murry [59]   John Middleton Murry (1889–1956). English literary critic and sometime partner of Katherine Mansfield, he introduced Finch's poems in a 1928 edition.

Now the jonquille [59]   Finch, "The Spleen," lines 40–41.

My lines decried [60]   Finch, "The Spleen," lines 79–80.

My hand delights [60]   Finch, "The Spleen," lines 83–86.

laughed at . . . Pope or Gay [60]   Some scholars believe that the character of Phoebe Clinket, who suffers from the "poetical Itch" in John Gay's, Alexander Pope's, and John Arbuthnot's satirical comedy *Three Hours After Marriage* (1717), is a caricature of Anne

Finch. *Bluestocking* is an eighteenth-century term for a female intellectual or a woman of letters.

Trivia [60]   John Gay (1685–1732), English poet and playwright, authored *Trivia, or The Art of Walking the Streets of London* (1716).

the Duchess [60]   Margaret Lucas Cavendish, duchess of Newcastle (c. 1623–1673).

Women live like Bats [61]   The conclusion of the first of seven speeches by and about women in Cavendish's *Female Orations* (1662).

Sir Egerton Brydges [61]   An English literary historian (1762–1837) who composed a preface to a 1814 edition of Cavendish's *Memoirs.*

Welbeck [61]   Cavendish's country house.

Dorothy Osborne's letters [61]   Dorothy Osborne, later Lady Temple (1627–1695), was famous for the letters collected in *The Letters of Dorothy Osborne to William Temple;* a 1928 edition was reviewed by Woolf.

After dinner wee sitt [62]   An excerpt from Osborne's Letter 19, undated but assumed to have been written on Sunday, May 8, 1653. The line quoted just after this is from Letter 18, also undated and assumed to have been written on Sunday, May 1, 1653.

Mrs. Behn [63]   Aphra Behn (1640–1689), English poet, playwright of some fourteen plays, and the author of *Oroonoko* (1688), which supposedly recounts Behn's earlier experiences in Surinam and protests against the institution of slavery. A onetime spy with a reputation for promiscuity, she was the subject of Vita Sackville-West's biography in 1927.

A Thousand Martyrs [63]   "A Thousand Martyrs I have made" and "Love in Fantastic Triumph sat" are two of Aphra Behn's poems that Vita Sackville-West quoted in her 1927 book on Behn.

Lady Dudley [63]   An obituary of Georgina, Lady Dudley, appeared in the *Times* on February 4, 1929.

Charing Cross Road [64]   London street famous for its bookshops.

Crusades or the Wars of the Roses [64]   The former were the expeditions undertaken to "liberate" Christian holy sites from Muslims and Jews, from 1095 to 1270, with an estimated dead of 1.5 million; the latter, a series of English civil wars fought from 1455 to 1485 between the Houses of Lancaster and York (red and white roses, respectively), with an estimated 100,000 casualties.

Pride and Prejudice ... Wuthering Heights [64]   Novels by Jane Austen, George Eliot, Charlotte Brontë, and Emily Brontë.

Eliza Carter [65]   A translator of the classics and friend of Dr. Samuel Johnson, Eliza Carter (1717–1806) was a prototypical bluestocking or literary woman and the subject of one of Woolf's early reviews.

Westminster Abbey [65]   The burial place of many English kings and queens as well as famous poets and statesmen.

supreme head of song [65]   An allusion to the Greek poet Sappho (b. 610 B.C.) in Algernon Charles Swinburne's "Ave Atque Vale" (1868), an elegaic poem in memory of Charles Baudelaire (line 18). In a letter dated January 1, 1929, Woolf argued that "Sappho was not a unique writer but supported by many other poetesses. That I think until the late eighteenth century was never the case in England."

Miss Emily Davies [66]   The founder of Girton College, Emily Davies (1830–1921) was a suffragist and a pioneer in women's education. In the various drafted versions, Emily Davies plays a larger role, often with Anne Clough and Leigh Smith (see, for instance, Rosenbaum 162, 185–86, 191).

women never have an half hour [66]   From Nightingale's *Cassandra,* mentioned above.

Grace Poole's laugh . . . [68]   In Charlotte Brontë's novel *Jane Eyre,* the heroine later discovers that the eccentric laugh she is hearing does not come from the servant Grace Poole but from the madwoman Bertha Mason Rochester.

St. John's Wood [69]   A northwest district in London where George Eliot lived out of wedlock with the literary critic George Henry Lewes (who was unable to obtain a divorce from his mentally ill wife). This made Eliot disreputable to some in her family and circle of acquaintances.

I wish . . . invitation [69–70]   Eliot's words here and subsequently appear in *George Eliot's Life,* authored by the man she married after Lewes's death, J. W. Cross (II, 112).

Tolstoi [70]   The author of *War and Peace* (1865–69), Leo Tolstoy (1828–1910) was a prominent Russian novelist.

domed like the Cathedral of Saint Sofia [70]   Named for the female personification of Wisdom in the Bible, the Hagia Sophia is a domed basilica completed in A.D. 537. Woolf visited Constantinople (now Istanbul) and viewed the cathedral in 1906.

Rochester [72]   The brooding and mysterious hero of *Jane Eyre* (1847).

female novelists . . . of their sex [74n]   Michèle Barrett has pointed out that Woolf omits to mention that the author was her friend Desmond MacCarthy, who cited her along with Jane Austen in his original remarks.

Browne . . . De Quincey [75]   Besides the literary men already mentioned above, Woolf lists authors famed as prose stylists. Thomas Browne (1605–1682); John Henry Cardinal Newman (1801–1890), Laurence Sterne (1713–1768), Charles Dickens (1812–1870), and Thomas De Quincey (1785–1859) composed tracts, essays, theological works, and fiction.

The ape . . . to be sedulous [75]   According to Alice Fox, the phrase derives from Robert Louis Stevenson describing his training in literature through imitation; he "played the sedulous ape to Hazlitt, to Lamb, to Wordsworth, to Sir Thomas Browne, to Defoe, to Hawthorne, to Montaigne, to Baudelaire, and to Obermann" (in his essay "A College Magazine," 1910).

Balzac [75]   Honoré de Balzac (1799–1850) was a prominent French novelist.

Gibbon [75]   Edward Gibbon (1737–1794) was the author of *The History of the Decline and Fall of the Roman Empire* (1776–88).

Jane Austen looked . . . and laughed [76]   In a manuscript version, Woolf quotes a passage from *Pride and Prejudice* as an example of Jane Austen's shapely sentences:

She examined into their employments, looked at their work, & advised them to do it differently; found fault with the arrangement of the furniture, or detected the housemaid in negligence; & if she accepted any refreshment, seemed to do it only for the sake of finding out that Mrs. Collins's joints of meat were too large for her family (Rosenbaum 182).

interruptions there will always be [77]   In a manuscript version, Woolf adds, "*Nor are they always harmful, for most people of course, write too much*" (Rosenbaum 182).

Chapter Five

Vernon Lee's books [78]   Under the pseudonym Vernon Lee, Violet Paget (1856–1935) wrote essays, novels, and books about art.

Gertrude Bell's books [78]   The archaeologist and travel writer Gertrude Bell (1868–1926) wrote *Persian Pictures,* which was reprinted in 1928.

Mary Carmichael [78]   Another allusion to the Scots ballad, this name also evokes Marie Carmichael, the pseudonym used by Marie Stopes, an early birth-control activist, who published a work entitled *Love's Creation* in 1928.

Emma and Mr. Woodhouse [79]   The heroine and her father in Jane Austen's novel *Emma* (1816).

Sir Chartres Biron [80]   The chief magistrate in the obscenity trial against Jonathan Cape, publisher of Radclyffe Hall's *The Well of Loneliness* (1928). Considered a classic in lesbian literature, *The Well of Loneliness* was put on trial on November 9, 1928, and the book was declared obscene on November 16. Although both Woolf and Vita Sackville-West had qualms about the literary quality of the novel, they would have testified on its behalf if allowed to do so.

Diana of the Crossways [81]   An 1885 novel by the English author George Meredith (1828–1909), a friend of Woolf's father.

Racine [81]   Jean Racine (1639–1699) wrote popular plays.

They shared a laboratory together . . . [82]   In *Women & Fiction,* after the words "they shared" appears a break because, the narrator informs us, the pages of the book "had stuck" together, giving her an opportunity to reflect on "the inevitable policeman; the summons; the order to attend the court; the dreary waiting; the Magistrate coming in with a little bow; the glass of water; the counsel for the prosecution; for the defense; the verdict; this book is ~~called~~ obscene; & flames rising, perhaps on Tower Hill, as they consumed <that> masses of ~~print~~ paper. Here the pages came apart. Heaven be praised! It was only a laboratory" (Rosenbaum 114).

Sir Hawley Butts . . . *Burke or Debrett* [84]   While the first might be of Woolf's devising, Burke and Debrett composed reference works of genealogy and the peerage about the British aristocracy.

Whitaker [84]   *Whitaker's Almanac* plays a major role in Woolf's later treatise *Three Guineas* (1938). Founded in 1868 by Joseph Whitaker, the *Almanac* contained general data about the population, governments, and commerce of England and the United States.

Cowper . . . *Browning* [85]   William Cowper (1731–1800) was a popular British poet; Percy Bysshe Shelley (1792–1822), a British Romantic poet; the French man of letters Voltaire (1694–1778) wrote philosophy and criticism; Robert Browning (1812–1889) was a British poet best known today for his dramatic monologues.

Sir William Joynson Hicks [85]   An English Conservative politician (1865–1932), he was also an evangelical religious figure and the home secretary who had banned *The Well of Loneliness* by Radclyffe Hall.

Thrale [85]   Hester Lynch Thrale (1741–1821) was a close friend and hostess to Dr. Samuel Johnson. After her husband's death, she married Gabriel Piozzi, an Italian musician, much to the distress of Johnson. Her home was called Streatham Park.

battle of Balaclava [88]   A disastrous blunder in the Crimean War, it was made famous by Tennyson's "Charge of the Light Brigade" (1854).

King Edward the Seventh [88]   Edward VII was born in 1841.

chemist [88]   British term for druggist.

Juvenal . . . Strindberg [89]   Both the Roman satirist Juvenal (c. 60—127) and the Swedish playwright August Strindberg (1849—1912) were famous for misogynist portraits of women.

Mr. Woodhouse and Mr. Casaubon [89]   The former is the father of the heroine in Jane Austen's *Emma;* the latter, the husband of the heroine in George Eliot's *Middlemarch* (1872). Both are satirized for their self-absorption.

You can't do this and you shan't do that! [92]   A sentence reminiscent of Charles Tansley's in *To the Lighthouse* (51).

Chapter Six

Whitehall [96]   London street housing chief offices of the British government.

Coleridge [97]   Samuel Taylor Coleridge (1772—1834) claimed that "a great mind must be androgynous," and his remark was recorded in *Table Talk* of September 1, 1832. In the manuscript version, Woolf considers "what one means by an androgynous, conversely by a gunandros mind" (Rosenbaum 186).

The Suffrage campaign [98]   With support rising throughout the nineteenth century, the campaign for women's suffrage established the Women's Social and Political Union in 1903; suffragist methods included legal and illegal protests, and of course eventuated in the establishment of women's right to vote.

Miss Clough and Miss Davies [100]   Anne Jemima Clough (1820–1892) organized for women's education and became principal of Newnham College; Emily Davies (1830–1921), mentioned previously, became mistress of Girton College.

Mr. Galsworthy and Mr. Kipling [100]   John Galsworthy (1867–1933) and Rudyard Kipling (1865–1936) were popular English novelists at the time. Extended in the typescript, the attacks on Galsworthy and Kipling are prefaced by Woolf's faulting women "who held up magnifying glass instead of ordinary glass when men looked at them for so many years; and thus indirectly led to the foundation of the Indian Empire, and- <*the establishment of* > the British Dominions- <*Colonies*>" (Rosenbaum 188).

old Jolyon's head [101]   The patriarchal head of the Forsyte family in Galsworthy's *The Forsyte Saga* (1922).

Sir Walter Raleigh's letters [101]   The critic and essayist Sir Walter Raleigh (1861–1922) was the first professor of English Literature at Oxford.

the Duce [101]   The leader, a term for the Italian Fascist Mussolini. In a manuscript version, there is an extended analysis of posters, flags, banners, and Fascist corporate leaders in Italy (Rosenbaum 190).

the truth to Mr. Greg [102]   Mentioned earlier, William Rathbone Greg (1809–1891), whose "Why Are Women Redundant?" (1862) referred to the "problem" of single women.

Ben Jonson [102]   Playwright, actor, and poet laureate, Ben Jonson (1572–1637) is best known for his plays *Volpone* (1606) and *The Alchemist* (1610).

Whitaker's Almanac [104]   Whitaker's "Table of Precedency" lists the formal social ranking of everyone in Britain from Sovereign to Gentleman, from Queen to Wife of Gentleman. This order was established by an act of Parliament passed by Henry VIII.

Commander of the Bath . . . Master in Lunacy [104]   The former is the third-highest order of chivalry in the British honors system, established by George I in 1725; the latter refers to the role created by the Australian Lunacy Act of 1878, an appointment to undertake the supervision of estates of insane persons in New South Wales.

Sir Arthur Quiller-Couch [105]   Holder of the King Edward VII Professorship of English Literature at Cambridge from 1912 until his death in 1944. The title Woolf quoted consists of his first series of lectures published in 1916. Leonard Woolf and George Rylands edited and published his volume *A Lecture on Lectures* (1928) as the first in the Hogarth Lectures on Literature series.

Byron, . . . Morris, Rossetti [105]   Lord Byron (1788–1824) was a Romantic poet; Walter Savage Landor (1775–1864), a minor British Romantic poet; Matthew Arnold (1822–1888), a Victorian poet and cultural critic; William Morris (1834–1896), a socialist, artist, and poet; Dante Gabriel Rossetti (1828–1882), a poet associated with the Pre-Raphaelites.

Saul . . . Painters [106]   Robert Browning composed both *Saul* and *The Ring and the Book*, while John Ruskin (1819–1900) was a leading art critic and the author of *Modern Painters* (1843).

Atropos [106]   The female Fate in Greek mythology who cuts the thread of life.

John Clare [106]   A working-class poet (1793–1864), John Clare eventually was institutionalized for his madness.

James Thomson [106]   A British poet (1834–1882), famous for his melancholy; laudanum is a drug containing opium.

Sappho . . . Lady Murasaki [108]   The legendary first classical poet who lived on the island of Lesbos (b. 610 B.C.); Murasaki Shikibu (978?–?1026), the Japanese author of the masterpiece *The Tale of Genji*.

Piccadilly [108]   A crowded shopping area in London where five busy streets merge.

La Recherche du Temps Perdu [108–9]   Woolf uses the original French title of Proust's series of novels (*Remembrance of Things Past*).

Sir Archibald Bodkin [110]   Director of public prosecutions during the obscenity trial of Radclyffe Hall's *The Well of Loneliness*.

Mr. John Langdon Davies [110]   Michèle Barrett notes that Woolf exaggerates, for the quotation reads, "And if children cease to be altogether desirable, women cease to be altogether necessary."

Sir Sidney Lee [111]   The author of the *Life of William Shakespeare* (1898) was a prominent scholar (1859–1926).

Milton's bogey [112]   A much interpreted phrase referring in part to *A Room*'s earlier allusions to Milton. Alice Fox points out the significance of three Miltonic passages: Eve's statement to Adam that "God is thy law, thou mine: to know no more / Is woman's happiest knowledge and her praise"; the definition of woman as "a fair defect of Nature"; and the line "He, for God only; she, for God in him" (all from *Paradise Lost*).

SUGGESTIONS FOR FURTHER READING:
Virginia Woolf

Editions

The Complete Shorter Fiction. Edited by Susan Dick. 2nd ed. San Diego: Harcourt, 1989.

The Diary of Virginia Woolf. Edited by Anne Olivier Bell. 5 vols. New York: Harcourt, 1977–84.

The Essays of Virginia Woolf. Edited by Andrew McNeillie. 6 vols. [in progress]. San Diego: Harcourt Brace Jovanovich, 1986–.

The Letters of Virginia Woolf. Edited by Nigel Nicolson and Joanne Trautmann. 6 vols. New York: Harcourt Brace Jovanovich, 1975–80.

Moments of Being. Edited by Jeanne Schulkind. San Diego: Harcourt, 1985.

A Passionate Apprentice: The Early Journals, 1897–1909. Edited by Mitchell A. Leaska. San Diego: Harcourt, 1990.

Biographies and Reference Works

Briggs, Julia. *Virginia Woolf: An Inner Life.* San Diego: Harcourt, 2005.

Hussey, Mark. *Virginia Woolf A to Z: A Comprehensive Reference for Students, Teachers, and Common Readers to Her Life, Works, and Critical Reception.* New York: Facts on File, 1995.

Kirkpatrick, B. J., and Stuart N. Clarke. *A Bibliography of Virginia Woolf.* 4th ed. Oxford: Clarendon, 1997.

Lee, Hermione. *Virginia Woolf.* New York: Knopf, 1996.

Marder, Herbert. *The Measure of Life: Virginia Woolf's Last Years.* Ithaca, NY: Cornell University Press, 2000.

Poole, Roger. *The Unknown Virginia Woolf.* 4th ed. Cambridge: Cambridge University Press, 1995.

Reid, Panthea. *Art and Affection: A Life of Virginia Woolf.* New York: Oxford University Press, 1996.

General Criticism

Abel, Elizabeth. *Virginia Woolf and the Fictions of Psychoanalysis.* Chicago: University of Chicago Press, 1989.

Bazin, Nancy Topping. *Virginia Woolf and the Androgynous Vision.* New Brunswick, NJ: Rutgers University Press, 1973.

Beer, Gillian. *Virginia Woolf: The Common Ground.* Ann Arbor: University of Michigan Press, 1996.

Cuddy-Keane, Melba. *Virginia Woolf, the Intellectual, and the Public Sphere.* Cambridge: Cambridge University Press, 2003.

DiBattista, Maria. *Virginia Woolf's Major Novels: The Fables of Anon.* New Haven, CT: Yale University Press, 1980.

Fleishman, Avrom. *Virginia Woolf: A Critical Reading.* Baltimore: Johns Hopkins University Press, 1975.

Froula, Christine. *Virginia Woolf and the Bloomsbury Avant-Garde: War, Civilization, Modernity.* New York: Columbia University Press, 2005.

Guiguet, Jean. *Virginia Woolf and Her Works.* New York: Harcourt Brace Jovanovich, 1965.

Harper, Howard. *Between Language and Silence: The Novels of Virginia Woolf.* Baton Rouge: Louisiana State University Press, 1982.

Hussey, Mark. *The Singing of the Real World: The Philosophy of Virginia Woolf's Fiction.* Columbus: Ohio State University Press, 1986.

———, ed. *Virginia Woolf and War: Fiction, Reality and Myth.* Syracuse, NY: Syracuse University Press, 1991.

Majumdar, Robin, and Allen McLaurin, eds. *Virginia Woolf: The Critical Heritage*. Boston: Routledge, 1975.

Marcus, Jane. *Art and Anger: Reading Like a Woman*. Columbus: Ohio State University Press, 1988.

———, ed. *New Feminist Essays on Virginia Woolf*. Lincoln: University of Nebraska Press, 1981.

———, ed. *Virginia Woolf: A Feminist Slant*. Lincoln: University of Nebraska Press, 1983.

———, ed. *Virginia Woolf and Bloomsbury: A Centenary Celebration*. Bloomington: Indiana University Press, 1987.

———. *Virginia Woolf and the Languages of Patriarchy*. Bloomington: Indiana University Press, 1987.

McLaurin, Allen. *Virginia Woolf: The Echoes Enslaved*. Cambridge: Cambridge University Press, 1973.

McNees, Eleanor, ed. *Virginia Woolf: Critical Assessments*. 4 vols. New York: Routledge, 1994.

Minow-Pinkney, Makiko. *Virginia Woolf and the Problem of the Subject: Feminine Writing in the Major Novels*. New Brunswick, NJ: Rutgers University Press, 1987.

Phillips, Kathy J. *Virginia Woolf Against Empire*. Knoxville: University of Tennessee Press, 1994.

Roe, Sue, and Susan Sellers, eds. *The Cambridge Companion to Virginia Woolf*. Cambridge: Cambridge University Press, 2000.

Ruotolo, Lucio. *The Interrupted Moment: A View of Virginia Woolf's Novels*. Stanford, CA: Stanford University Press, 1986.

Silver, Brenda R. *Virginia Woolf Icon*. Chicago: University of Chicago Press, 1999.

Zwerdling, Alex. *Virginia Woolf and the Real World*. Berkeley: University of California Press, 1986.

SUGGESTIONS FOR FURTHER READING:
A Room of One's Own
(in addition to the works cited in the introduction)

Abel, Elizabeth. "The Poetics of Hunger, the Politics of Desire: Woolf's Discursive Texts." In *Virginia Woolf and the Fictions of Psychoanalysis*, 68–83. Chicago: University of Chicago Press, 1989.

Ezell, Margaret J. M. "The Myth of Judith Shakespeare: Creating the Canon of Women's Literature." *New Literary History* 21.3 (1990): 579–92.

Fernald, Anne. "*A Room of One's Own:* Personal Criticism and the Essay." *Twentieth Century Literature* 40.2 (Summer 1994): 165–89.

Folsom, Marcia McClintock. "Gallant Red Brick and Plain China: Teaching *A Room of One's Own.*" *College English* 45.3 (1983): 254–62.

Fox, Alice. "Literary Allusion as Feminist Criticism in *A Room of One's Own.*" *Philological Quarterly* (Spring 1984): 145–61.

Jacobus, Mary. "The Difference of View." In *Reading Woman: Essays in Feminist Criticism*, 27–40. New York: Columbia University Press, 1986.

Kamuf, Peggy. "Penelope at Work: Interruptions in *A Room of One's Own.*" In *Signature Pieces: On the Institution of Authorship.* Ithaca, NY: Cornell University Press, 1988.

Marcus, Jane. "'A Very Fine Negress.'" In *Hearts of Darkness: White Women Write Race*, 24–58. New Brunswick, NJ: Rutgers University Press, 2004.

―――. "Sapphistory: The Woolf and the Well." In *Lesbian Texts and Contexts: Radical Revisions,* 164–79. Edited by Karla Jay and Joanne Glasgow. New York: New York University Press, 1990.

Marcus, Laura. "Woolf's Feminism and Feminism's Woolf." In *The Cambridge Companion to Virginia Woolf.* Edited by Sue Roe and Susan Sellers, 209–44. Cambridge: Cambridge University Press, 2000.

Moi, Toril. "Who's Afraid of Virginia Woolf?: Feminist Readings of Woolf." In *Sexual/Textual Politics,* 1–18. New York: Methuen, 1985.

Moran, Patricia. " 'The Cat Is Out of the Bag'; and It Is a Male: Desmond MacCarthy and the Writing of *A Room of One's Own.*" In *Essays on Transgressive Readings: Reading Over the Lines.* Edited by Georgia Johnston, 35–55. New York: Mellen, 1997.

Rosenman, Ellen Bayuk. "Sexual Identity and *A Room of One's Own:* 'Secret Economies' in Virginia Woolf's Feminist Discourse." *Signs* 14.3 (1989): 634–50.

Stimpson, Catharine R. "Woolf's Room, Our Project: The Building of Feminist Criticism." In *Virginia Woolf.* Edited by Rachel Bowlby, 162–79. London and New York: Longman, 1992.

Walker, Alice. "In Search of Our Mothers' Gardens." In *In Search of Our Mothers' Gardens.* San Diego: Harcourt Brace Jovanovich, 1983.

Woolf, Virginia. *Women & Fiction: The Manuscript Versions of* A Room of One's Own. Transcribed and edited by S. P. Rosenbaum. Oxford: Blackwell, 1992.

Zwerdling, Alex. "Woolf's Feminism in Historical Perspective" and "Anger and Conciliation in *A Room of One's Own* and *Three Guineas.*" In *Virginia Woolf and the Real World,* 210–70. Berkeley: University of California Press, 1986.

Virginia Woolf Annotated Editions

Top Woolf scholars provide valuable introductions, notes, suggestions for further reading, and critical analysis in this paperback series. Students reading these books will have the resources at hand to help them understand the text as well as the reasons and methods behind Woolf's writing.

Between the Acts
Annotated and with an introduction by Melba Cuddy-Keane
978-0-15-603473-9 • 0-15-603473-5

Jacob's Room
Annotated and with an introduction by Vara Neverow
978-0-15-603479-1 • 0-15-603479-4

Mrs. Dalloway
Annotated and with an introduction by Bonnie Kime Scott
978-0-15-603035-9 • 0-15-603035-7

Orlando: A Biography
Annotated and with an introduction by Maria DiBattista
978-0-15-603151-6 • 0-15-603151-5

A Room of One's Own
Annotated and with an introduction by Susan Gubar
978-0-15-603041-0 • 0-15-603041-1

Three Guineas
Annotated and with an introduction by Jane Marcus
978-0-15-603163-9 • 0-15-603163-9

To the Lighthouse
Annotated and with an introduction by Mark Hussey
978-0-15-603047-2 • 0-15-603047-0

The Waves
Annotated and with an introduction by Molly Hite
978-0-15-603157-8 • 0-15-603157-4

The Years
Annotated and with an introduction by Eleanor McNees
978-0-15-603485-2 • 0-15-603485-9

Each volume includes a preface by Mark Hussey, professor of English and women's and gender studies at Pace University, and editor of *Woolf Studies Annual*.

Harcourt | HARVEST BOOKS
www.HarcourtBooks.com